D1622285

Edward's Twilight

Joseph Veillon

ISBN: 1-4751-6215-4
ISBN-13: 9781475162158

Dedication

For my friend, Jennifer, who introduced me to *Twilight*. Without her encouragement and friendship this book would never have been finished.

CONTENTS

PROLOGUE

Vampire Edward Cullen was once an honest-to-goodness, card-carrying, vile, bloodsucking vampire – the vampire of your most horrible nightmares. A *real* vampire. Sadly, Stephenie Meyer made Edward an inhumanly beautiful, *sparkling* vampire in a teen romance novel called *Twilight.* Edward Cullen, former mean, nasty, authentic vampire, was reduced to a sanctimonious parody of a yuppie Greek god. Edward's vampire reputation was ruined and he now lives in hiding. Told by Edward Cullen himself, in the voice of his alter ego, Edwin Dullen, the following account is Edward's version of the *Twilight* story.

Chapter 1.

A DANGEROUS GUY

It was a perfect January morning in the small, somewhat eccentric community of Full Moon, Washington, population 3120 souls, and home of the annual Full Moon Halloween Festival, a week-long celebration of goblins, ghouls, and all manner of spookiness featuring interactive tours of Full Moon's cemeteries and haunted houses, an Invisible Man look-alike contest, the *Shaun of the Dead* Zombie Walk, the wildly popular Grave Robbers Scavenger Hunt, and the Dead by Dawn Horror Movie Festival, which attracts scores of horror movie fans from all over the world. The temperature hovered just above freezing and an unremitting drizzle of icy rain fell from the dismally gray sky. The weather forecast called for a howling wind and several inches of snow overnight. It looked to be a great day.

In my room, getting ready for school, I spent three hours bathing, whitening my teeth, manicuring my nails, styling my hair, moisturizing, and applying sunscreen. Looking inhumanly beautiful takes a lot of work. After splashing on some Old Spice cologne and putting on my red *I Love Transylvania* t-shirt and my brown *Count Chocula* hoodie, I jumped into my silver 1985 Yugo and sputtered off to school. Arriving at the distinctive and unique main building of Full Moon High School, I marveled at how it had the unmistakable look and nostalgic feel of an institution that could be nothing else but a small town high school, clearly recognizable and obvious even without the sign out front. I turned into the school parking lot at the corner of

Michael Street and Myers Avenue, parked in the space marked RESERVED FOR PRINCIPAL, and made my way through the usual mob of vampire groupies crowded around the school entrance.

The halls were crowded with students buying, selling, and trading an illicit assortment of cheat sheets, stolen exams, forged excuses, internet term papers, pirated movies, illegally downloaded music, and counterfeit *Twilight* merchandise. The entire school hummed with anticipation and gossip about the new girl—Jezebella Penguin—the chief's daughter, who was returning to Full Moon after years of exile in the parched and sundrenched desert of Arizona.

The chief is Gnarly Penguin, the legendary Chief Game Warden for the western Olympic Peninsula of Washington state. Chief Penguin and his deputies, Eben, Marlowe and Iris, spend most of their time investigating the numerous wolf sightings and incidents of deer poaching in the forest around Full Moon, both of which have strangely increased during the past two years. Chief Penguin, more depressed than a child on Santa's naughty list at Christmas, has been grumbling for days about the return of his daughter to Full Moon. "I'll have to move Jezebella's stuff from the garage back into her room and give up my game room," he grumbled to his friends upon learning of his daughter's imminent return.

At lunch, I was talking with my brothers and sisters at a table we had taken away from some freshmen students when the entire cafeteria suddenly hushed. All eyes turned to the entrance as she walked into the room, a stunningly beautiful, slender, dark-haired, bronzed goddess of the desert, who strolled into the room like a Victoria's Secret lingerie model, and then, just as suddenly, everyone in the cafeteria issued a collective groan of disappointment and the riotous din of lunchroom chatter resumed. It was only Miriam Seward, who had recently moved to Full Moon from Moab, Utah. Her dad is the new doctor at the insane asylum out on Renfield Road just north of town.

Several seconds later the entire cafeteria abruptly went silent once again as everyone's attention returned to the entrance, where, in the doorway, stood the stunningly ordinary and unremarkable, slender, green-eyed, dark-haired new girl, with pasty skin the color of soymilk, or maybe Swiss cheese—Jezebella Penguin. For a short moment that seemed to go on forever, you could have heard a cotton ball drop to the floor. After five seconds of uncomfortable silence during which the entire room rudely gawked while Jezebella stood in the door relishing everyone's worshipful admiration of her plainness, the spell was broken and the room quickly filled once again with the loud ruckus of teenage gossip and idle conversation.

However, something was wrong. I could not read Jezebella Penguin's mind. The cafeteria was a swirling kaleidoscope of many dozens of thoughts. My mental voyeurism normally allowed me to know the most private and personal of thoughts—savoring any intimacy or suffering endless mundane trivia. But Jezebella gave me nothing. No discernible thought of any kind issued forth from her mind. In fact, I was quite troubled because I could not read anyone's mind today. I did not understand it. Could it be that I was some delusional freak whose mind did not work right, hearing voices in my head that were not real? *"Holy Telepathic Blooper!"* The realization dawned on me all of a sudden. I can't read minds. The mind reading vampire is in that *other* book.

Jezebella made her way to a table near the salad bar, walking through the room as if she knew that every pair of eyes in the place was closely following her every move. She pulled out a chair, and with all the grace and poise of a drunken carhop on roller skates, she missed the seat completely and plopped spastically onto the floor. She didn't exactly have that lithe dancer's step. Picking herself up because no one offered to help her, Jezebella sat down at the table with an elegance that belied her evident clumsiness and smiled as if she had not just suffered a mortifying coordination malfunction in front of half the school. This girl was good. She has obviously had practice with this sort of thing.

Jezebella sat at the table with Jessica Vain, a self-centered blonde who once had the shameless audacity to ask *me* out on a date. Sitting next to Jessica was Maxwell Newton, called Max by his parents and teachers but known as Fig by everyone else in town. His parents own the local sporting goods store, Lost Expedition Outfitters. Fig is absolutely the most irritating boy in school. He and Jessica will undoubtedly be voted Most Annoying Couple at prom. The group also included Angelica Wicca and Elliot Shih Tzu. Angelica is a really cool but slightly weird girl who is reputed by some to be a witch. Elliot is famous among the students of Full Moon High School for hiding a spy camera in the faculty lounge and catching the two health teachers, Ms. Crabbe and Mr. Burns, in an after-hours romantic tryst. Elliot has been known as the eyes and ears of this place ever since. Angelica and Elliot are both on the staff of the Full Moon High School newspaper, *The Howling,* which won the 2004 Elvira award for its series on cheesy vampire movies.

As Jezebella listened to her new friends conceitedly talk about themselves, she looked in my direction every few seconds, no doubt attracted by my flawless inhuman beauty. I tried not to stare, but this uncoordinated, ghostly apparition from the desert intrigued me. I had grown accustomed to the idea that the girls at Full Moon High School were not good enough for me, and I had not expected to be interested in this girl of such unexceptional plainness, but she had some undefined quality that piqued my curiosity. Every time she looked my way, she caught me staring at her with an intense look that seemed to unnerve her. But I could not help myself; sometimes I'm just as ill-mannered and uncouth as everyone else. The bell signaling the end of lunch rang, and so I dumped my half-eaten apple into the trash and headed off to biology class.

As I sat at my desk waiting for class to begin, I amused myself by playing *Castlevania* on my laptop computer and daydreaming about Jezebella, remembering her wickedly inept fall to the floor and superb recovery of dignity. A slight commotion interrupted my idle musing and I was surprised to see Jezebella Penguin enter the room. *"Holy Transylvania!"* I mumbled under my breath, giving silent thanks to Stephenie, Melissa, and Catherine because the only empty seat in the room was right next to mine. Pulling out my pocket mirror, I quickly checked my look and popped several breath mints into my mouth. Jezebella spoke briefly with the teacher, Mr. McFeely, and I saw her deftly dodge his hand and give him a hard scowl as she turned and walked toward my desk.

As Jezebella sat down next to me, the air stirred and her luscious scent swirled around me. She smelled like tomato juice, my favorite fruit, or vegetable, whichever it really is. I was instantly afflicted with a lust a thousand times more intense than my natural affinity for human blood and my sudden desire to taste her was nearly uncontrollable. I instinctively recoiled and leaned away from her, my entire body contorting in fitful spasms in response to the assault of her scent, while my face morphed into a grimace of confused torment that looked like that famous painting called *The Scream*. My body perversely twisted this way and that way in a frenzied corporeal tantrum that resembled a chaotic jumble of the thriller dance, the funky chicken, the twist, the running man, and the hokey pokey. I finally collapsed atop the desk and lay drooling like a rabid dog. I must have looked like an unhinged lunatic.

My fiendish hunger for Jezebella was urgent. Her scent was sweeter than any human I had ever smelled and I eventually dared to creep a few inches more toward her side of the table. My self-control quivered as I struggled to choke back my desire and restrain my desperate urges. I was deranged with longing and frenzied with sinful desire for this luscious human creature. As my body convulsed with lust I could feel myself channeling the spirits of the great vampire masters—Lugosi, Lee, Hamilton, Murphy, Nielsen, Count von Count.

The sweet fragrance of her blood excited my most base instincts and my most contemptible desires. I would definitely need to see Father Karras for confession. I slowly moved ever closer to her. Even while gripped in the fervent throes of arousal, I felt terrified of these urges that overshadowed me with a foreboding sense of doom. In the space of mere seconds, a few molecules of Jezebella's tomato juice scent had reduced me to a sordid, mindless monster, loathsome and shameful in the weakness of my hunger. I swallowed hard and inched closer.

I fought for control. I could not allow my wretched frailty to ruin this chance to impress Jezebella Penguin with my *savoir-faire, je ne sais quo, panache,* and *sang-froid.* If only I could control my urges, I would beguile her with my vampire charisma and sophistication. She would be powerless to resist my vampire hypnosis.... I mean charm. She would become mine. With my eyes closed, I leaned ever closer to her, letting the sugary perfume of her aroma wash over me.

Wait. No! What is she doing? Sniffing her hair? Curses, swearwords, and unholy vexations! She smells it, that putrescent rotting aroma of the dead known in the world of perfumery as the vampire bouquet. Despite bathing in gallons of cologne and slathering on gobs of deodorant, covering up nearly eighty-seven years of decomposed putrefaction is nearly impossible. Maybe she won't realize the odor is coming from me. After all, we *are* in a biology laboratory.

Then it happened. Fate intervened. Murphy's Law was invoked. The orbits of the earth and moon shifted out of alignment. Yin and yang spun out of balance. The sun went dark. I leaned too far towards Jezebella and gravity did its ugly work. Desperate to stop my fall, I frantically reached for the only thing available—Jezebella Penguin—shamefully grabbing her by the arm and pulling her down with me into the supermassive black hole of the abyss. We crashed with a hard thud. Jezebella landed beneath me with a look of stunned horror and disbelief on her face. "I'm really quite dangerous, Jezebella. You should probably stay away from me. I'm not good for you. I'm a dangerous guy," I said as I picked myself up from the floor without offering to help her up.

As I collected myself and recovered from my embarrassment, I stepped over Jezebella and hurriedly fled the scene of my mortification. My mind raced like a stopped clock. I realized instantly that Jezebella Penguin was meant to be my eternal soul mate. It was fate preordained that we should be together. I was suddenly and hopelessly in love, in lust, infatuated, obsessed, enraptured. She would make me whole. Jezebella Penguin would complete me.

Chapter 2.
MAKING FRIENDS

What a beautiful morning—icy cold, cloudy, and snowing. The snow was coming down steadily in wonderfully light, fluffy, unique flakes, not at all like that heavy, mushy cotton swab stuff. My brothers and I had a snowball fight this morning before leaving home. My sisters refused to leave the house until we promised to behave. We had planned to lure them outside into an ambush, but threats of gruesome retaliation were made and the girls reminded us of Rosalie's grisly revenge on Royce and of how Alice had coolly separated James' head from his body. We prudently gave up the ambush idea. After arriving at school, we continued our snowball battle in the parking lot, but we disappeared into the building when an errant snowball broke a classroom window.

Later at lunch, I was sitting with my family at a table we had again stolen from some freshmen, when Jezebella entered the cafeteria along with Selene Lycan and went to the food bar. She filled her tray with chicken nuggets, a slice of pepperoni pizza, two oatmeal cookies, and a root beer.

As Jezebella turned away from the food bar, she bumped the Cullen kid and caused him to spill soup all over his shirt. Walking away completely oblivious of the disaster, she gave me a look of pure unadulterated scorn. I was mortified, horrified, and vilified. With a whole week to get over things, I had hoped that Jezebella would have forgotten our unfortunate first encounter. After all, she had suffered only a mild concussion and a few bruises.

Jezebella's table was populated with her group of new fake friends, which today also included Lenore Poe, Selene Lycan, Tyson Fryer, and Victoria Stewart. Lenore Poe writes weird poetry and is president of the Dead Poets Society. Selene Lycan is a bit mysterious and no one knows much about her, but she is rumored to be some kind of martial arts ninja. Tyson Fryer has failed driver education class three times and works weekends as a pizza delivery driver. Victoria Stewart, although a ginger-haired beauty, is a somewhat possessive girl and some would say even a bit of a stalker. The motley group at the table looked like they could be actors in a *Twilight* movie parody. All during lunch, Jezebella kept turning to stare at me, her eyes shooting daggers deep into my cold, undead heart. She looked as though she wanted to stab me in the eye with her pencil.

How could I woo Jezebella if she was going to be so hostile? This was an unforeseen complication and I could not help feeling apprehensive about our upcoming biology class. It was important that I be on my best behavior and make a good impression on Jezebella today. I sprayed myself down with Old Spice and some androgynous pheromones and slicked my hair with extra gel. For good measure, I sent a tray of aphrodisiac foods to Jezebella's table. For the rest of the day all of the girls kept smiling and winking at me and handing me their phone numbers, all except Jezebella.

After taking my seat in biology, I pulled out my computer and checked my Facebook page. Stephenie Meyer turned down my friend request for the tenth time and blocked me. Bummer. I don't think she likes me. While waiting for class to begin, I pondered the philosophical and metaphysical conundrum that the dual temptations of bloodlust and carnal desire might lead me into dangerous circumstances with Jezebella. Considering my reaction to her last week, I began to doubt the wisdom of courting Jezebella Penguin, but I found myself powerless to resist her vanilla charms and colorless personality. The combination of my fascination with her unadorned persona and my instinctual lure to her rich and alluring tomato juice scent fueled a totally illogical but overwhelming desire for Jezebella. I just could not help myself.

Jezebella entered the room and took her seat next to me. Her scent blitzed me like a crowd of illegal immigrants scrambling after a dropped green card. This time I was prepared. I whipped out my new battery powered personal fan, pointed it at Jezebella, and clicked the "on" switch. Nothing happened. I clicked the switch again. Nothing happened. I pried the fan open with my pointed vampire fingernails. Damn! No batteries. My animalistic vampire urges were stirring. Forgetting the disaster of last week, I was already inching closer to Jezebella's side of the table, leaning toward her and relishing her sweet scent. I wanted her more than anything I had ever wanted in all my life. Nevertheless, before I could romance Jezebella Penguin, I had to get my vampire cravings under control. Yoga might help. I assumed the Lotus position on top of my desk and sat there chanting "Om" for several minutes.

"Hello Jezebella," I sang in my most musical, lyrical voice. "My name is Edwin Dullen. I didn't have a chance to introduce myself before knocking you down last week."

"Hello," Jezebella hesitantly answered after a few seconds with clear apprehension in her voice. She looked wary and eyed me suspiciously. "I'm surprised you have the nerve to speak to me. You knocked me down and left me crippled on the floor. *You gave me a concussion!*"

"I'm truly sorry about that Jezebella," I replied. "I was only trying to save myself."

"I had to spend two days at home with my dad taking care of me and helping me to the bathroom. I'm seventeen years old. Do you have any idea what that was like?"

"The instinct for self-preservation is a very powerful thing," I answered. "Won't you please accept my apology and be my friend?"

"I'm not done with you yet. What were those bizarre contortions and weird looks on your face all about? You looked like you were having convulsions. Are you sick? You're not contagious with anything, are you?"

"Well, I do have a type of blood disorder," I admitted.

"Just keep it to yourself. And why did you keep slinking so close to me?" she demanded. "You invaded my personal space. It was creepy." Revulsion coated her every word.

"I'm so sorry, Jezebella. Can't we please be friends?" I asked, involuntarily slinking a little closer.

"You do seem a little better today, like you're only having little convulsions, but you're invading my space again. Just what is with you?" She pulled a stun gun from her book bag and pointed it directly at me. "Back off, Edwin."

"You smell like tomato juice and it drives me crazy," I quickly explained while retreating to my side of the table.

"You'd better not be making fun of me," Jezebella warned as she waved the stun gun at me. "I know how to use this 150,000 volt shocker-gun-thingy. I practiced a dozen times on the neighbor's cat, so I know what I'm doing."

"I swear, Jezebella, I'm not making fun of you."

"Well, okay. Now that we have some boundaries established, I'll think about grudgingly and temporarily accepting your apology, but that doesn't mean we're friends. What do you mean about me smelling like tomato juice? I don't like tomato juice."

"It's very difficult to explain. You're so plain and I don't understand why I'm so attracted to you. Those wild gymnastic contortions were merely an outward physical manifestation of the inner conflict between the part of my instinctual nature that wants to kill you and the intellectual part of me that doesn't want to be a homicidal monster."

"What in the world are you talking about?" Jezebella asked, obviously annoyed.

"Jezebella, couldn't we just be friends, hang out, have fun, and hope for the best?"

"We could try, Edwin, but you know that any relationship between us would almost certainly be doomed to inevitable failure and adolescent heartache. After all, you're so inhumanly beautiful and so way out of my league."

"Come on, Jezebella, live a little."

"Hey, what's up with your eyes? Last week they were black and today they're green."

"I must have gotten new contacts. Yes. That's it. I got new contacts."

"Where have you been? You missed a whole week of school. Principal Forks fired Mr. McFeely and we had some cool substitute teachers. On Wednesday, Dr. Kevorkian gave a fascinating lecture on poisons, and on Thursday Mr. Dahmer did some dissection demonstrations. It is just amazing how real looking they can make those practice body parts. Best of all was Friday when Mr. Romero gave a presentation on the scientific principles behind the theories that zombies and reanimation of the dead are actually possible."

"Zombies are kind of creepy, but I would have totally enjoyed that discussion," I admitted.

"So, where were you last week?" Jezebella persisted.

"I was embarrassed about knocking you down and I thought you hated me, so I left town for a few days."

"You left town because you thought I hated you?"

"Well, yes—partly."

"I did hate you for a bit, but leaving town sounds so excessively over-the-top. You could have just sent me chocolates or flowers, or simply apologized. FYI, chocolates are preferred," Jezebella replied, running her tongue around the rim of a chocolate covered cherry and slowly sucking it into her mouth.

"How do you like Full Moon? The cold and constant rain must be hard for you, considering that you've been living in the desert for so long."

"Actually, I love the blustery, icy wetness of Full Moon. The bitter winter bleakness and cheerless misery complement my perpetually melancholic mood."

"You like this weather?" I asked in surprise.

"I *love* this weather. The heat in Phoenix is blistering, and it's difficult being gloomy and depressed when the sun shines all the time," Jezebella responded. "I love that for most of the year the Full Moon weather is cloudy, raining, or snowing."

"All of this green must be strange for you, though."

"Oh, no. I like the green. Everything in Arizona is just so brown, like on an alien planet—Mars or maybe Venus."

"So, you don't miss Phoenix?" I asked.

"Not really. Full Moon is actually pretty cool. My dad bought me a new car and a lot of guys ask me out on dates."

"The rumor around school is that you once lived in Full Moon."

"Yes. I was conceived during a power outage, at exactly two minutes and seventeen seconds past midnight on a cold, snowy Christmas Eve morning, and born 263 days, 21 hours, 34 minutes, and 12 seconds later right here in Full Moon, Washington. My mother moved away with me when I was just a snot-nosed little brat. We left because she couldn't deal with the weirdness of Full Moon anymore. Mom moved us to Roswell, New Mexico because of its UFO connection. Mom was once abducted by aliens and subjected to a bizarre medical examination with some very intimate probing. She said the experience was out of this world and she wanted to meet more aliens."

"That sounds very weird. Did you like Roswell?"

"It was okay, I guess. Mom worked as a waitress at the Uranus Café next door to the Close Encounters Motel. The whole town is alien central. They even have a UFO festival every July."

"Full Moon has a Halloween festival every October," I informed Jezebella. "Ours is the biggest Halloween festival in the world."

"I know. Mom says that the festival attracts a lot of weird screwballs, as if Full Moon doesn't already have enough strange characters."

"How did you end up back in Full Moon?"

"Mom waited five years for the aliens, but when they didn't show up in Roswell we moved to Phoenix. She had heard about the Phoenix UFO sightings and thought it would be a good place to meet aliens. The aliens never came to Phoenix either, at least not the extraterrestrial kind."

"So, then you moved to Full Moon?"

"Mom met a professional crossword puzzle solver and decided to move to Florida with him. Florida has the largest population of crossword puzzle solvers in the nation. I'm not stupid. I knew that I wouldn't fit in with their nomadic crossword puzzle solver lifestyle, moving from newspaper to newspaper, always talking over my head in vowels and consonants. That's when I decided to come live with my dad in Full Moon. What else have people been saying about me?"

"You've actually been quite a popular subject of bathroom graffiti, lunchroom gossip, and teacher's lounge rumormongering ever since word got around about your return. Most of the boys in school were betting that you would be a sizzling hot sun goddess with an awesome tan."

"I am so sorry to disappoint," Jezebella replied, sticking her tongue out at me.

"I think that you will find nearly all 161 human males and several of the females at Full Moon High School to be definitely interested in you, tan or no tan."

"Would that include you?" Jezebella asked with a teasing twinkle in her eye. "By the way, I love your *Bite Me* medallion. I like people who say what's on their mind. I have a pink t-shirt with *Kiss Me* embroidered on the front in big red letters."

"How do you get along with your dad?" I quickly asked. "You've been gone a long time."

"Gnarly and I have mostly been apart for seventeen years and we have never really spent much time together, so he feels totally comfortable and relaxed with me suddenly in the house full time. Gnarly and I are both very talkative, verbose even, so we got caught up on the past seventeen years in about ten minutes. One of the best things about Gnarly is that he hovers and is always watching out for me. He built himself an outhouse in

16

the woods behind our house so that I wouldn't have to share the bathroom. Can you believe that? It was so sweet of him to think of me."

"That was very considerate of your dad. Sounds like you're adjusting to Full Moon quite well."

"Things are great. My room even seems like it hasn't been touched since I left. I did discover that Gnarly doesn't really have any culinary skills, so I'm definitely taking over kitchen duty. Last night Gnarly was going to eat plain Fruit Loops for supper, but I stopped him and poured milk on those Fruit Loops for him. I also went shopping and stocked the kitchen with plenty of microwave dinners, frozen pizza, chips, peanut butter, and Gnarly's favorite food—fish sticks. Gnarly will be in gastronomic heaven. I don't know how he has managed all these years without me."

"Your dad is really lucky that you know how to cook," I remarked.

"What about you, Edwin? I heard that you and your family moved here from Alaska."

"We moved to Full Moon two years ago. Before that, we lived for a time with friends in Talkeetna, Alaska."

"I thought your Alaskan friends lived in Denali?"

"There was a lot of talk in those *Twilight* books about Denali, but in reality there is no town or village named Denali anywhere in Alaska. To Alaskans, Denali refers to Mount Denali and the surrounding park. I don't know where those Alaskan vampires in that *Twilight* book really lived. Our Alaskan friends actually live just outside Talkeetna, which is quite an eccentric, off-the-wall, quirky little town. We fit in there very nicely."

"Is that where you've been for the past week?"

"Yes. Talkeetna is my home away from home."

"Tell me about your family, Edwin."

"The big guy who looks like he could eat you is Emrick. He's really just an overgrown Teddy Bear at heart and he tells the scary children's stories during the Halloween festival. Rachel is the sullen looking blonde with the perpetual scowl on her face. Rachel *will* eat you if you cross her. The hyperactive, edgy looking guy is Neville. He's a bit unstable because other people easily influence his moods. Neville's disposition has been known to change in the blink of an eye. Allison is the delusional brunette."

"Why do you call her delusional?"

"She thinks that she can see the future."

"What about your parents?"

"Argyle is a renowned hematologist. He studied under the eminent Dr. Peter Cushing of Bucharest, Romania. Carmilla is a very talented plastic surgeon. She practiced in Hollywood, so she has a lot of experience making people look younger than their true age."

"Your parents sound really cool, Edwin."

At that moment, the bell rang and I jumped up and swiftly bolted from the room. Even as it drew me to her, Jezebella's exquisite tomato juice scent threatened to undo me. Her astounding plainness simply *dazzled* me.

Chapter 3.
SAVING JEZEBELLA

It snowed again during the night. By morning, several inches of white powder had blanketed the ground and the pavement was treacherous with ice. Conditions were just right for some inept klutz who had not stayed in bed to slip on an icy sidewalk or driveway. Despite the stimulating learning environment of Full Moon High School, I was not eager to get to school this morning, so I drove around the parking lot seventeen times before finally parking in the space marked RESERVED FOR PRINCIPAL. I noticed that during the night someone had painted a mural of very colorful graffiti on a fence alongside the school parking lot. It seems that Full Moon must have its very own nighttime patrons of the arts.

Even though being near Jezebella had been easier yesterday, the lure of her tomato juice scent was still very powerful. Considering the danger of being in her company and the fact that my league was so far above her league, the smart thing for me to do would be to avoid Jezebella Penguin completely. However, I'm too weak and spoiled to do the smart thing. I'm powerless to resist her plainness. I must have her.

I was talking with my brothers and sisters next to my car when Jezebella arrived and parked only four car spaces over from us. Gnarly had bought Jezebella a brand new, gleaming red 2005 Ford Mustang GT as a coming home present. It was the finest car I'd ever seen. When she got out of her car Jezebella looked our way and smiled, but then she bumped her head on the door and the smile instantly disappeared. Jezebella's attention was then drawn to her tires, and she obviously noticed for the first time the snow chains on her tires. I was dumbfounded that Jezebella could be so oblivious as to have driven all the way to school unaware of their presence. Snow chains are really loud and clunky. Could she really be that clueless?

"There's your girl, Edwin," Rachel teased. "You should go over and say hello."

"Shut up, Rachel. You're not funny," I retorted. Argyle had told the family about my reaction to Jezebella and there had been quite a discussion about the incident. Everyone had previously experienced the reaction to human scent, so I expected that I would be entitled to a huge amount of sympathy and understanding, but all I got was a lot of rather irritating taunting and harassment. Everyone seemed to agree with Argyle that running off to Alaska was an excessively melodramatic and theatrical response to the situation. Neville said that if I had simply thought to invite Jezebella to a birthday party he would have been happy to handle the problem.

"She looks awfully thin and undernourished," Emrick snickered. "The next time you see her in the cafeteria you should buy her something to eat."

"Yes, invigorate her blood a little. She looks a bit anemic," Rachel added, slowly skimming the tip of her tongue along her upper lip.

"Edwin, if you want a human girlfriend, why don't you choose one of the really pretty girls like Miriam or Selene?" Neville asked.

"Yes, Edwin. Jezebella is so plain. She would really stand out as different from us," Allison added. "People would ask questions."

"We could tell people that Jezebella is a distant cousin from a different branch of the family," Emrick suggested.

"A *very* distant cousin," Rachel added.

"No. That wouldn't work," Allison said. "We would have to say that Jezebella was adopted."

"Adopted? Like people wouldn't see through that scam," Rachel declared. "Besides, an addition to the family would just encourage more gossip about incestuous siblings."

I looked up and rolled my eyes, and that's when I saw it. The morning news had reported that an explosion aboard the International Space Station had launched a million dollar space toilet into orbit around the earth with a reentry trajectory that would bring it down in the ocean somewhere off the coast of the Olympic Peninsula. Observing the flaming trail of the meteoric crapper, I realized with horror that someone had made a slight calculation error and that the interplanetary toilet was only seconds away from impact with the very spot presently occupied by Jezebella Penguin. I launched into a sprint and covered the four car spaces between us in no less than forty seconds. It all seemed as if I was spacewalking through a dream. Everything moved in dawdling slow motion, just like it happens in the movies.

Just before I reached Jezebella, she looked up and scrunched her face into a look of sudden, panicked comprehension of her impending doom. Crashing into Jezebella, I pushed her out of the way and sent her rolling, tumbling, and flipping across the parking lot, the hollow pop of her head as it bounced off the ground echoing in the still air. Just as Jezebella came to a stop several yards away, the errant space potty crashed into the very spot where she had stood only milliseconds before, pulverizing the parking lot and excavating a crater deep enough to hold a dozen Volvos. Thankfully, Jezebella's car was unscathed.

Shaken and a little bruised, Jezebella lay on her back, staring at me in confused disbelief. I had saved her. I was Jezebella's Superman and Hulk rolled into one. I was Jezebella's hero—I was her superhero.

"You…. you were…. over there…. by your car," Jezebella managed to stammer, looking dazed and utterly bewildered. "How…. did you…. reach me so fast?"

"Really now, Jezebella; is that the first thing you would ask?" I admonished. "I think not."

"Wha…. what?" she asked in woozy befuddlement.

"I'm just saying that most people who had just been saved from being crushed by a speeding space toilet would say something different."

"Like…. what?"

"Like 'what just happened,' 'get off me,' 'OMG,' 'what the hell,' 'am I dead?' or even 'thanks.' But, 'how did you reach me so fast' would not be the first thing out of my mouth."

"But, how…. how *did* you reach me so fast?" she inanely persisted.

"Jezebella, you were only four cars away from me. I was right there."

"Wha…. What are you talking about?" she interrupted.

"I can see that your learning curve is a bit steep. I was practically right next to you. It's not that big a deal. You're confused. You hit your head when I knocked you down. You're in shock."

"My head does have a hollow ring to it right now, but I'm not confused. I know what happened," she insisted.

"Jezebella, you *are* confused. I saved you from being squashed by a crashing space toilet. There's nothing more to it."

"No. There is more. You covered those four car spaces in forty seconds. You have superhuman speed. I know it. Why won't you tell me the truth?"

"OMG! Jezebella. In the movie, it may have looked as if I came from all the way across the parking lot, but in the book it was only four car spaces. Forty seconds for that distance is practically crawling. Let it go."

"I know what I saw, Edwin."

"That's just it, Jezebella. You didn't see anything. You were looking up at that flaming space toilet with an 'OMG I'm doomed' look on your face. You hit your head and now you're confused. You probably have a concussion."

"I'm going to be stubborn and unreasonable, Edwin. I am not letting this go."

"You should let it go Jezebella, for your own good. Trust me; I'm not a good friend for you. You should stay away from me. I'm a dangerous guy."

"I'm not going to let this go, Edwin. I may not be the smartest person, but I can be obstinate and pigheaded. I won't talk to you for weeks. I'll pretend you don't exist."

The school counselor, Mrs. Strode, and about two dozen students quickly converged on the scene, with everyone shouting and talking excitedly all at once. There were calls for an ambulance and a fire truck. Someone shouted that NASA should be notified. No one noticed as I discreetly crawled on my hands and knees to the edge of the crowd and inconspicuously made my way from the scene. I wanted the full spotlight of attention to be on Jezebella.

Chapter 4.
HELLO STEPHENIE

It was Thursday, the third day of March. Jezebella and I had not spoken to each other for five weeks. Jezebella had been typically unreasoning and headstrong, rejecting my perfectly logical and self-serving explanation that her perception of events was confused, jumbled, and befuddled because of her head injury. Jezebella was carried away that day by paramedic trainees who had her locked in a neck brace and wrapped up like King Tut's mummy by the time they reached the hospital. Needless to say, Jezebella was exceedingly annoyed, irritated, and infuriated with me.

Sitting next to Jezebella in biology class during this silent war of wills has been incredibly awkward. Jezebella made her annoyance with me evident every day by sitting with her back turned to me and by unplugging my computer right in the middle of my daily session of *Vampire Sims*. Her friends have mostly attributed the tension between us to yet another oddity, peculiarity, or idiosyncrasy of Edwin Dullen. Adding to my torture, Jezebella's tomato juice scent continues to excite my unbridled blood lust, and each hour spent next to her has been an agonizing test of willpower. Only with a herculean effort of self-control have I been able to resist dragging Jezebella off into the woods behind the school and draining her body of blood.

Driving down Full Moon Avenue after school, I spotted Jezebella's gleaming red Mustang parked in front of the Love at First Bite Cafe. I decided at that moment that it was time to end this ridiculous feud. If I could mend this quarrel between us, Jezebella would realize how unreasonable she has been and see just how brilliant and fabulous I really am, and then I could make her mine. We are destined to be together. I pulled into the lot, parked next to her car, dinged her fender when I threw open my door, and went inside. Jezebella was sitting at a front table having a hazelnut coffee and staring absentmindedly out the window at passing traffic. She must have seen me come in. It was a good omen that she didn't run out the back door.

"Hello, Jezebella." I spoke the greeting with uncertainty, anxious about what her response might be. "May I join you?"

She looked up and gave me a hard stare for several seconds before speaking. "I didn't see you come in. What are you doing here Edwin?"

"I'm asking if I may sit with you."

"Let me make sure I understand this correctly. You push me down and give me another concussion, a sprained ankle, a broken middle finger, and several bruises. Then you completely ignore me for five weeks, as if I don't even exist. And now, you want to have coffee with me?" she ranted, holding up her broken middle finger for me to see.

"Actually, I would prefer a glass of warm tomato juice," I said, sitting down across the table from Jezebella. "Considering recent events, I should remind you that it would be more prudent if we were not friends. In fact, I'd like you to sign this waiver releasing me from liability in the event our relationship should have an unfortunate ending."

"Are you brain damaged, Edwin? Have you been breathing formaldehyde fumes during biology class?"

"Can't we be friends, Jezebella?"

"Since you've twice failed to kill me, are you now trying to irritate me to death?"

"I'm trying to be nice and make amends, Jezebella."

"You've been very rude to me, Edwin. Your behavior during these past weeks gave me the distinct impression that you were not interested in me."

"I only avoided talking to you because I didn't want to argue with you. It wasn't that I'm not interested in you. And, for the record, you have been equally rude to me. After all, I did save your life."

"Maybe I was and maybe you did, but you were rude to me first. I only wanted you to answer my questions. It was a simple-minded request."

"I knew you would bring that up and confuse the issue. It's not as simple as you think, Jezebella."

"Then why did you come in here? Why don't you just leave me alone?"

"It's complicated."

"Try me, Edwin. I'm sure I can keep up."

"Look, Jezebella, here's the thing—it's not that I'm not interested in you—it's that I shouldn't be interested in you. But I do want to be with you."

"Decode that for me, Edwin. I don't speak schizophrenia."

"I like you, Jezebella, but in the grand scheme of the universe we probably aren't meant to be friends."

"That is so much better, Edwin. Things are now as clear as the muddled plot of a silly teenaged girl-vampire-werewolf love triangle in a dream-induced novel."

"I'm just trying to say that I adore and worship the ground you walk on, but that it would be better if we were not together.

In fact, it would be better if we were not pals, chums, buddies, or friends of any kind."

"*Great Jekyll and Hyde, Edwin!* You keep saying that you want to be friends, but then you change personalities and tell me it would be better if we stay away from each other. You're maddening, as if you have multiple personality disorder. Just tell me in plain English, what are you trying to say?"

"I want to be friends with you Jezebella, but my feelings are conflicted because I'm really not a good friend for you. It's just that relationships don't usually work out well for me. I can be rather.... intense."

"*Holy obfuscation, mystification, and incomprehension, Edwin!* You may be complicated and intense, but you're probably also insane. *Blessed Christina and Saint Dymphna, rescue me from this lunatic!*"

"Jezebella, you are downright ridiculous."

"And you are utterly absurd, Edwin." Then, after a long pause, "Why do you want to be friends with me?"

"Because you're so interestingly humdrum and unexciting," I replied.

"Interesting? Humdrum? Unexciting? You certainly have a way with words when you're trying to impress a girl."

"It's more than that, Jezebella. You're not like the popular or fashionable girls."

"Oh, thanks so much. That just totally made my day."

"I didn't mean it that way, Jezebella. It's just that your plainness stimulates an insane craving that draws me to you. I *am* trying to resist you, but I have this inhumanly powerful attraction to you."

"You are very weird and slightly insane, Edwin. Say, your eyes were green. Today your eyes are blue. What's the deal?"

"It must be the lights," I answered.

"Listen, Edwin. Some of us are going to the beach Saturday. Come with us."

"Who are you going with?"

"Jessica, Fig, Angelica, Elliot, Miriam, Selene, Sara Conner, Salem Lott, and that girl whose brother is in the FBI, Samantha Molder."

"Which beach?" I asked.

"We're going to Amity Island Beach at the end of Voorhees Road out at La Push. Come with us, Edwin. It sounds like a fun place. Angelica says there's shark watching and I want to go surfing."

"I don't know, Jezebella. Emrick and I were planning to go hiking and collect butterflies this weekend. He wants to add a few more to his collection."

"Oh come on, Edwin. Come to the beach with us."

"It sounds like fun, but I promised Emrick. Watching the big guy catch butterflies is the most fascinating thing I've ever seen. Besides, Jezebella, I'm really quite dangerous. If you were smart you would avoid me."

"No one ever accused me of being smart. Anyway, I like living on the edge. I wish you were coming. If you change your mind, everyone is meeting in front of Barlow Antiques in the Lost Expedition Outfitters shopping plaza."

"Okay. Enjoy surfing with the sharks, but be careful. There have been recent reports of sharks biting people without playing that *Jaws* shark attack music first."

"Hey, isn't that Stephenie over there behind that laptop?" Jezebella asked.

Joseph Veillon

"Yes, that's her," I confirmed. "Let's leave before she sees us," I said, rising from my chair and putting money on the table for our drinks and a nickel tip.

"Don't you want to say hello?"

"No. Not after she made my character such a namby-pamby wimp," I said as we discreetly made our way to the door and outside to the parking lot.

"Edwin, don't you feel even a little guilty about dodging Stephenie? After all, she is our creator. If not for her, we would not exist."

"That is exactly my point, Jezebella. If Stephenie had not written us into that literary blasphemy of hers, we would not be doomed to an existence of endless ridicule and disparagement."

"I guess you're right, Edwin. We will always be mocked and disrespected, except by all those Twilighters. I really don't know what they see in us."

"Jezebella, we must face reality and accept our fate. We will always be known above all else for our roles in that mind-numbing forgery of literature. We have been cursed to bear the burden of literary mediocrity for all eternity."

"I know. Our characters were just so unimaginative and uninteresting," Jezebella said with tears welling up in her eyes.

"You're much more perceptive than I thought, Jezebella. Our characters were very superficial and one-dimensional."

"It's sad, Edwin. We could have been so much more."

"Yes. We certainly could have been," I mused. "Both of our characters could definitely have been written with much more depth and personality. We were clearly short-changed."

"People say that *Twilight* is a love story, but our main attraction for each other was based on little more than our mutual lust. We didn't have any kind of intellectual connection," Jeze-

30

bella said. "You were also very arrogant and possessive, Edwin. You were practically a stalker."

"And yet, you were crazily obsessed with me," I retorted.

"Yes. I was madly obsessed with you. After only a few weeks, not only was I willing to leave my family and friends, give up my dreams, and sacrifice my self-esteem, but I was also ready to forfeit my humanity and even my very life in order to spend eternity with a manipulative, controlling, and emotionally distant vampire with anger issues."

"Don't forget vain, snobbish, and condescending," I added.

"You have a lot of issues, Edwin. If your character wasn't so inhumanly beautiful and perfect I would never have become involved with you."

"How can you say that, Jezebella? We had the perfect relationship."

"Edwin, what we had in *Twilight* was an unhealthy, disturbingly obsessive relationship masquerading as a romance. I can't believe that I was so pathetic."

"I'm sorry, but that's the way Stephenie wrote our characters, and they called her a literary phenomenon, even a literary luminary, Jezebella."

"Fine, she's a luminous literary…. whatever, but my character was still totally pathetic. I was such a poor example for girls in so many ways. I wish that I could have been a more positive role model," Jezebella said, her cheeks wet with tears.

"Again, you're quite observant," I remarked, handing her a fresh tissue.

"Now I'm depressed, Edwin. I'm going to need years of psychotherapy to get over this."

"I'm depressed too, Jezebella. I feel so pointless and unfulfilled."

"Edwin, I really need to get home now."

"Okay. I'll see you tonight…. I mean next week," I said as I helped Jezebella into her car. "Have fun with your friends at the beach."

Chapter 5.

DEVIL'S HARBOR

School was relatively uneventful today. Salem Lott found a mushy glob of unknown matter in his stew at lunch and caused a minor turmoil when he spit it out and a dollop of the gooey sludge landed on the front of Principal Forks' favorite shirt. The school cafeteria is infamous for its mystery food. The only other notable incident of the day occurred in gym, when Jezebella somehow tripped a girl while standing still in line and caused her to sprain an ankle.

In biology class I was able to talk with Jezebella for only a few minutes before our blood typing exercise. I knew that all of that free-flowing blood would be dangerously tempting and I had considered cutting class, but I decided that it was worth the risk to get a whiff of Jezebella's delectable, freshly drawn blood. The thought made me lightheaded with anticipation.

"How was your trip to the beach?" I asked.

"The weather was perfect for a day at the beach. It was cold, it rained most of the day, and there was a wicked rip current."

"I see that you managed to not get eaten by a shark."

"I did manage to avoid the jaws of death, but we saw several sharks swimming just a few yards off the beach. A boy in my class named Brody Quint was paddling his kayak along the beach taking pictures of the sharks and he just disappeared. We came back from a hike and he was gone. Strange thing though, his car is still parked at the beach and he hasn't been in school."

"Are you doing anything after school today?" I inquired.

"I'm going to Devil's Harbor with Jessica and Angelica. They want to buy dresses for the dance Saturday. We're going to Morticia's Closet, a used dress boutique on the boardwalk."

"Are you dress shopping too?"

"No. I'm not going to the dance, but I want to criticize the dresses that Jessica and Angelica try on."

"You meant to say critique their dresses, didn't you?"

"No. I meant criticize their dresses."

"Don't you like dancing, Jezebella?"

"Oh, yes I do, but I'm pretty sure that my style of dancing would not be acceptable at Full Moon High School."

"That's a very curious statement. Just what is your style of dancing?"

"Well, I like dirty dancing. I'm very good at it, but it causes problems."

"I'm quite certain that the administration of Full Moon High School, the PTA, and the Full Moon High School Warriors for Jesus Society would all frown on dirty dancing."

"No, Edwin, not that kind of problem. At the dances, all of the boys want to dance with me, but their girlfriends hate me. Actually though, some of the girls want to dance with me too. But is it my fault that I'm such a hot dirty dancer?"

"That's very interesting, Jezebella. I never would have guessed that you were a dirty dancing aficionada."

"The only time my feet move in harmony is when I'm dancing."

"Will you be late tonight?"

"We plan to eat dinner at a French restaurant on the boardwalk called Le Petit Cochon, but I shouldn't be home late. Did you want to call or visit me tonight?"

Trying to follow Jessica's fast sports car along Highway 101 proved impossible. My Yugo had a top speed of only eighty-eight miles per hour and quickly fell far behind. Arriving in Devil's Harbor, I found Jessica's car parked on the dilapidated boardwalk, so I found a quiet corner next to the Quileute Pub where I could stand motionless and collect dust while waiting for the girls to finish shopping. Jessica and Angelica walked by me four hours later, but without Jezebella. They told me that Jezebella had gone to check out the Jonathan Harker Vampire Museum and that she planned to meet them for dinner at Le Petit Cochon.

The vampire museum was only a few blocks from the boardwalk, but some very unsavory characters could be found in the museum area after dark, so I dusted myself off and went looking for Jezebella to make sure that she was safe. By the time I reached the museum on Ripper Avenue it had closed and I used my superior vampire intellect to deduce that Jezebella must be walking back to the boardwalk. There were plenty of creepy characters and bizarre oddballs on the streets and the entire neighborhood had an eerie, unsettling atmosphere. It was a lot like watching *The Munsters* or *The Addams Family*.

I found Jezebella in front of Conliffe Antiques on Talbot Street. She was backed up against a wall, madly swinging her purse back and forth as she fought off an unruly gang of crazed adolescents. The frenzied horde of teenyboppers had Jezebella boxed in against the wall. Each one of them was reaching toward Jezebella with outstretched arms as if they were radioactive zombie children, and they were all chanting "Bella" repeatedly in a nonstop mantra of irrational adulation. I immediately realized that the situation was gravely serious. Jezebella was under siege by a mob of Twilighters.

I zoomed up to the curb and bounced my Yugo onto the sidewalk, forcing the Twihards to scatter. Leaping from the car, I crouched nervously behind Jezebella, peeking around her as I snarled and flailed my arms to scatter the pubescent muggers.

"Quick, get in the car before they regroup," I ordered.

"Where did you come from, Edwin?" she asked in a rush.

"There you go with your silly questions again."

"But, where did you come from?" Jezebella went on.

"Just get in the car Jezebella!" As I jumped into the car and pushed the accelerator to the floor, the Yugo sluggishly made a creeping escape along the sidewalk, bounced back onto the street, and crawled toward the boardwalk. "Those Twilighters were vicious! Are you okay?"

"Edwin, you're going the wrong way!" Jezebella shouted. "The boardwalk is in the other direction."

Imitating that scene from the movie, I slammed on the brakes and simultaneously spun the steering wheel, wanting the Yugo to spin around and reverse direction, except that it continued to spin around and around until I was too dizzy to see straight. Regaining my senses after a minute I stomped on the accelerator and the Yugo zoomed off like a drunken snail.

"That was a close call back there, Jezebella. They almost had you."

"They swarmed me when I came out of the Soylent Green Candy Shop down the block. I tried to run but I tripped and they cornered me at the antique shop."

"I'm sure that I saw some Twilight Moms in that crowd. We were lucky to escape in one piece," I said.

"I was so scared. Never before in my whole life have I been surrounded by a gang of wild Twilighters. It was terrifying. I felt like a teacher in public school. What are you doing here anyway, Edwin?"

"I followed you from Full Moon."

"There's no way, Edwin. The silver turtle could never keep up with Jessica's car," she taunted.

"I knew where you were shopping and I waited for you on the boardwalk. When Jessica and Angelica told me that you had gone to the vampire museum, I came looking for you."

"Why did you follow me, Edwin? Are you stalking me?"

"I just wanted to make sure that I knew exactly where you were, what you were doing, and who you were doing it with."

"Okay, just as long as you're not stalking me."

"Look, there's Jessica and Angelica." Jezebella's friends were just coming out of Le Petit Cochon on Merrin Street. I parked and we got out of the car.

"You ate dinner without me?" Jezebella both questioned and accused her friends.

"Well, yes, we totally did," Jessica answered. "You were off on your museum expedition and, like, you didn't come back. We assumed that you were, like, with Edwin."

"I'm so sorry Jezebella," Angelica added. "I know it was totally rude but we ate without you anyway."

"I cannot believe you ate dinner without me."

"We were totally hungry," Jessica replied. "We were, like, really starved."

"Weren't you worried about me?"

"Not really, but even if we did there's a twenty-four hour waiting period before we can report you missing. It only made sense for us to go ahead and have dinner."

"Oh, right. I forgot about that. I'll just get something at Hurl & Heave Burger and purge it on the way home."

"Actually, I'll drive you home if you stay and have dinner with me," I offered hopefully. You shouldn't suffer because your friends were inconsiderate. You should have a good meal."

"I.... guess so. That would be nice," Jezebella responded.

"That's so very thoughtful of you, Edwin," Angelica said.

"Yes, like, totally thoughtful," Jessica added.

"Okay. I'll see you at school tomorrow," Jezebella said to her friends.

Leaving Jessica and Angelica gushing and giggling on the sidewalk, we went inside the restaurant where an attractive waitress showed us to a table in a quiet corner with a nice view of Exorcist Island out in the bay. A song incoherently mumbled by that vampire actor guy from *Twilight*, Rob somebody, labored in the background.

"I'll be your waitress tonight," she announced as she handed us menus. "My name is Regan." I observed that she paid particular attention to Jezebella, hardly noticing me at all. "Would you like something to drink while you look over the menu?"

"I'd like a root beer," Jezebella said.

"I'll have a glass of warm tomato juice," I added.

"One root beer and one warm tomato juice coming right up," Regan replied, smiling warmly at Jezebella as she turned to get our drinks.

Jezebella shivered and wrapped her arms around herself. "Are you cold," I asked.

"A little," she replied.

"Here, take my jacket," I said as I stood up and helped her into my black leather bomber jacket with *I Live for Blood* embroidered on the back.

"Thanks, Edwin. Your jacket is very warm."

"What were you doing in that neighborhood," I asked Jezebella.

"I wanted to see the vampire museum."

"Is there any particular reason you wanted to visit the vampire museum?" I asked. "It doesn't get many visitors."

"I've been dreaming that a vampire sneaks into my room at night to watch me sleep."

"And that bothers you?" I asked.

"Maybe just a little. I like to sleep in the nude," Jezebella answered. I fought fiercely to hide my smile.

Regan returned with our drinks and some stale croissants, making eye contact with Jezebella but ignoring me completely. "Would you like to order now?" she asked.

"I'll have a sirloin steak please," Jezebella replied. "Very rare. Make it bleed. What do you want, Edwin?"

"I'll just have another warm tomato juice." Regan barely acknowledged my order, but winked at Jezebella as she tucked her notepad into a pocket and headed off in the direction of the kitchen.

"Edwin, I want to ask you something."

"Ask me anything."

"It's your eyes again. They were blue, but now they're hazel. Did you get a contact lens variety pack or something?"

"Yes. That's a very good explanation. I must have gotten a variety pack."

"You know, a weird thing happened at Amity Island Beach. I met a boy named Jody Silver Bullet. Meeting him gave me such a strange feeling. I was certain that I remembered him in the movie, but I didn't know him in the book. It was very confusing. He told me a bizarre story."

Joseph Veillon

"I know Jody Silver Bullet. His mother died in childbirth with his older brother. What kind of story did he tell you?"

"I just told you it was a bizarre story."

"What kind of story was it?" I asked again.

"Aren't you listening to me? It was a *bizarre* story."

"No, Jezebella. I meant what was the story about?"

"Oh. He told me an urban legend about shape-shifting werewolves running loose in the woods around Full Moon."

"You don't really believe in werewolves, do you? Would you believe me if I told you that Jody Silver Bullet is a werewolf and that on nights when the moon is full he transforms into a skanky beast, scratches himself in ugly places, and smells like an outhouse?"

"Werewolves could be real, Edwin. Haven't you ever seen *Teen Wolf* or those *Underworld* movies?"

"Actually, a lot of people in Full Moon believe the werewolf legend. People have been finding piles of smelly, shredded clothes in the woods for a couple of years now."

At that moment, Regan appeared with Jezebella's food and fresh glasses of root beer and warm tomato juice, which she set on the table before us, lingering for several seconds with her hand resting lightly on Jezebella's arm.

"Is there anything else you'd like?" Regan asked.

"I'm fine, thank you," Jezebella smiled.

"Okay sweetie. Just let me know if you change your mind," Regan offered, giving me the evil eye.

Cutting her steak into pieces, Jezebella stabbed a morsel with her fork and took a bite. As Jezebella chewed her meat, a bit of blood trickled from the corner of her mouth. She never looked more lovely or desirable.

40

"Edwin, at the museum I met a mysterious, pale-skinned woman named Lucy. She followed me all through the museum and finally slipped me this note just as I was leaving." Jezebella unfolded the note and laid it on the table for me to read.

The note read *Your Boyfriend Might be a Vampire if:*

He has a putrid, tomblike scent.

He is inhumanly beautiful and totally conceited.

He owns an "I Love Transylvania" t-shirt.

He owns a Count Chocula hoodie.

He wears a "Bite Me" medallion.

His eyes change color every few days.

He drinks warm tomato juice.

"The signs were so subtle and it didn't make any sense, but I thought about it a lot and finally figured it out. I know what you are, Edwin. At first, I thought you were just an annoying, clumsy computer nerd, but now I know the truth. You're an annoying, clumsy *vampire* computer nerd."

"You're smarter than most people think," I remarked.

"Thanks, Edwin."

"If I really was a vampire, would that scare you, Jezebella?"

"Well, only a little. You're a good vampire."

"Why do think that I'm a good vampire?"

"If you were an evil vampire, by now you would have bitten my neck, sunk your fangs into my jugular vein, sucked out all of my blood, and left my shriveled, lifeless body in the woods to rot and be eaten by maggots."

"I see. So you're convinced I'm a vampire."

"I'm absolutely, indisputably, unmistakably, and undeniably positive. Yes, I'm pretty sure that you're probably a vampire."

"But you can't prove I'm a vampire."

"Not beyond a reasonable doubt, not without question, not certainly, and not definitely, but I have persuasive circumstantial evidence that would hold up in any court, except maybe with the OJ jury. Besides, that crypt-like smell of yours is a dead, or undead, or maybe living dead giveaway."

Bogus, cheap, generic vampire scent neutralizer from Taiwan! I should have spent the extra two dollars for the premium brand from Transylvania, made for vampires by vampires.

"Edwin, I know that at this very minute you are vacillating between continuing your unfulfilling counterfeit existence and confessing the truth and coming out of the coffin. I promise that I won't tell anyone. I just want to know the truth to satisfy my own perverse curiosity."

"Jezebella, you really should let this go and stay away from me. I'm not good for you."

"I cannot just let it go and stay away from you, Edwin. I have no other options, and right now, I want nothing more than to be with you. You're my only ride home."

I signaled to our waitress that we were ready for the check. Regan hurried over and handed me a small tray with the check and two antacid tablets, the only attention she paid me during the entire evening.

"I hope everything was okay," she cooed to Jezebella. "You come back soon."

"Thank you," I said tersely as we got up to leave.

"Edwin, isn't the waitress supposed to be flirting with you, not me?"

"Yes, but she must be dazzled by my magnificence and unable to focus properly."

Outside, I walked Jezebella to my car, let her in, and then walked around and got in behind the wheel. I started the car and the puny engine pathetically whimpered to life. Cautiously checking for oncoming traffic, I slowly and warily eased into the street and drove into the night.

Chapter 6.

SECRETS REVEALED

Creeping through the light traffic of West Front Street, I turned right onto Highway 101 heading back to Full Moon, the lights of Devil's Harbor lingering endlessly in the rearview mirror.

"*Holy speed trap, Edwin!* Can't you drive any faster? You're only doing eighty."

"I'm sorry, but I'm going as fast as I can."

"I thought the dead traveled fast," Jezebella said in exasperation.

I inserted a disk into the CD player and Concrete Blonde's "Bloodletting" began playing.

"Wow! That is such a cool song. I can't believe you have that," Jezebella babbled.

"You like "Bloodletting?" I asked in amazement.

"Oh, yeah. "Bloodletting" is an awesome song."

"It's something of a theme song for me," I said. "What other songs do you like?"

"I'm really into Joan Jett right now. "I Want You," "You Drive Me Wild," and "Do You Wanna Touch Me" are all way cool songs.

"Oh, yeah. Joan Jett totally sends me over the edge," I said.

"Those songs describe my feelings perfectly," Jezebella hinted, giving me a mischievous smile as she played with the top button of her blouse.

Joseph Veillon

"I think "I Hate Myself for Loving You" is a cool song too," I replied, trying to ignore Jezebella's flirtatious hint, although I hoped she would continue.

"I like that one too. Please tell me, Edwin, are you really a vampire?"

"Only a few minutes ago you were absolutely, indisputably, unmistakably, and undeniably positive."

"I still am—I think—maybe. But I want to hear you say it, Edwin."

"Let me evaluate the situation. Beginning with our first conversation the week after I knocked you down in biology class, we have known each other for about six weeks, but we spent about five of those weeks not even speaking to each other. In addition, during the short time that we have been speaking, we have had only three actual conversations covering mostly super-ficial, frivolous, and meaningless trivia. We don't really know anything about each other. Yes, of course, Jezebella. Without doubt, I will tell you my deepest, darkest, most precious secret."

"Yes! Finally!"

"Yes, Jezebella, I am a vampire." I whispered the words hesitantly, hardly believing what I was doing.

"Say it again, Edwin."

"*I AM A VAMPIRE!*" I said, loudly and forcefully enunci-ating each word.

"Okay, Edwin. That time was just a little scary. You know, in *Twilight* you never really came across as a scary character."

"You don't think I was scary?"

"No. Not really. In the book, you mostly came across as a love-struck teenager who was confused, indecisive, and prone to overdramatizing. But you were a bit more menacing in the movie."

46

"Thank you. I hoped to appear menacing onscreen."

"You're welcome. Actually, in the movie you still had some issues with confusion and indecision, but not as much as in the book. There are some scenes in the movie where you briefly appear slightly dangerous and threatening."

"Thank you for that favorable review."

"You're quite welcome."

"Jezebella, don't you care that I'm a pompous vampire with unresolved personality, character, and temperament issues? Fig, Elliot, and Tyson are all available suitors. Considering my somewhat eccentric character quirks and erratic behavior, why would you want to be with me?"

"It's true. I could use and abuse any of them and trample their hearts at will, but hey, are you kidding? You do have a few adjustment issues, but you are totally inhumanly beautiful and perfect, and for some insane reason you want a plain, shallow girl like me. I know how to grab a good deal when it knocks me over."

"But doesn't it bother you that we have nothing in common?" I asked.

"Not at all. Just look at what our unnatural relationship did for *Twilight's* book sales," Jezebella replied.

"Jezebella, I've wanted you from the first day I smelled your fantastic tomato juice scent. That day in biology, you literally sent me over the edge, and I knew immediately that I must have you. Since then I have contemplated that I might be in love with you, but I soon realized that I was merely obsessed with you and that we would probably never have a truly meaningful relationship. That made it so much easier for me."

"Edwin, I can only describe what I feel in the sense that I tremble for my beloved. Thinking of you makes my heart quiver and my knees wobble. My collective soul yearns for your touch. Gosh, Edwin, are we declaring ourselves?"

"If you mean declaring our ridiculous obsession with each other, then yes, I think we are, but you are more obsessed with me than I am with you."

"I am not," Jezebella retorted.

"Yes, you definitely are," I said. "I could easily walk away from this relationship, but you can't. Without me, your life would be no more than a series of blank pages."

"Edwin, I want to know your true vampire secrets."

"You mean like never let a vampire get wet and never feed a vampire after midnight?" I teased.

"What are you, a vampire or a gremlin? Seriously, Edwin, I want the scoop on your real vampire secrets like sunlight, coffins, garlic, mirrors, crucifixes, and graveyards."

"Well, only the truly old school vampires still use coffins. I like my comfort. A good mattress is better than a layer of moldy dirt in a cramped coffin any day, even if the dirt does come from the old country."

"So, you sleep then?"

"Of course we sleep. Just check out any Dracula movie," I answered, making the sign of the cross thirteen times.

"Why did you just cross yourself thirteen times? Are you Catholic?"

"No. We idolize Dracula and hold him in very high esteem. He was the first vampire to truly establish his place in folklore, history, literature, and cinema. Dracula is true vampire royalty—there are no others, only pretenders."

"What about garlic?"

"Vampires throughout history have been repelled by garlic. Would you want to kiss someone with garlic breath?"

"Do vampires have reflections in mirrors?"

"Of course we do. How else would we admire and appreciate our physical beauty and perfection?"

"Are you repelled by crucifixes?"

"Not at all. In fact, we have a rather large cross on a wall in our house."

"Do you hang out in graveyards?"

"Graveyards are very quiet and peaceful and are great places for meditation."

"Is it true that you can't enter a home unless invited?"

"Only in the movies."

"Can you turn into a wolf like the vampires in old movies?"

"The ability of vampires to transform into wolves is an ancient power that we no longer use. No vampire has attempted such a transformation in over a thousand years. In fact, because we consider the lycanthropes to be such vile creatures, most vampires will not even acknowledge that such an ability ever existed. The very thought of a vampire defiling himself in that way is abhorrent."

"What about having skin as hard as stone?"

"The idea of a vampire with a buff, toned, chiseled body of nearly indestructible stone with venom for blood is completely absurd and preposterous. The whole idea completely disregards not only time-honored literary tradition but also the fundamental and irrefutable laws of biology, biochemistry, and physics. You can Google it."

"But what about fantasy, Edwin?"

"Throughout history, vampires have always been flesh and blood creatures. Although traditional vampires are murderous fiends, they mostly retain the human qualities they possessed before becoming vampires, except for being dead, or undead, or living dead, or whatever. That humanness is one reason that vampires are scary. The human familiarity of vampires is what disturbs people. It creeps people out. Vampires may be immortal, but in many ways, they are also quite mortal. If you're a vampire fan you can probably easily imagine being a vampire, but I would bet that you can't imagine yourself as a creature with skin like stone."

"I see your point, Edwin."

"The vampires in *Twilight* would have been more interesting if they had been more humanlike, more vulnerable and fallible. Less perfect flesh and blood vampires would have been more believable. After all, what little interest those *Twilight* vampires did have was due to their human qualities, not their superficial perfection."

"You're so smart, Edwin. I never thought about it 'that way."

"Besides, if my skin was as hard as stone I could never have gotten my ear pierced and I wouldn't have been able to get this cool *ED Loves JP* tattoo."

"That is a way cool tattoo. Look at mine," Jezebella said, twisting around in her seat and pulling the waist of her jeans down for me to see the *Wolves Rule* tattoo on her hip.

"Say, just what team are you on, anyway?" I asked.

"I guess I have been a bit ambivalent about that," she responded.

"Don't you want to ask me about blood drinking, Jezebella?"

"Well, yes, no, and maybe."

"Does that subject make you nervous?"

"It doesn't make me nervous, but thinking about blood does make me feel uneasy, anxious, tense, and a bit queasy."

"Blood is life."

"Do you…. drink human blood?" Jezebella asked nervously.

"Is there any other kind?" I teased, seeing the concern on her face. "My favorite blood is type O."

"Edwin! My blood is type O." Jezebella's eyes were wide with apprehension.

"Yummy, no wonder I'm so attracted to you," I teased again, making a show of licking my lips. "Having type O blood makes you a universal donor," I added, giving her a wink.

"Don't tease me!" she demanded.

"In actual fact, Jezebella, all vampires drink blood, and virtually all vampires drink *human* blood. There is no such thing as a vegetarian vampire. It's simply our nature to drink human blood. Why should we resist what we are? Life is stressful enough. However, things can sometimes be a bit problematic."

"What do you mean?"

"I once knew a vampire who developed a rare disorder where his body could absorb nourishment only from the blood of virgin human females."

"What happened to him?"

"He died of starvation," I replied.

"I thought vampires were immortal."

"In theory, vampires can live forever, but vampires can die. Immortal is not absolute and is not the same as indestructible."

"Speaking of mortality, how old are you, Edwin?"

"I'm seventeen."

"I mean how old are you, really?"

"I'm a little over one hundred years old."

"Do you really drink human blood, Edwin?" Jezebella asked cautiously, after several long seconds of quietly processing my last statement.

"Here's the thing about blood. Some vampires break with tradition and get their blood from animals, but my family and I consider ourselves humane and civilized, so we drink only human blood. We also don't want the SPCA and PETA folks making trouble for us."

"How do you get human blood? You don't kill people, do you?"

"*Holy homicide!* No, Jezebella. We get our blood compliments of Full Moon Community Hospital. Donated blood has a shelf life and must be disposed of when it reaches its expiration date, just like milk at the grocery store. We don't even have to steal it. Argyle supervises the blood bank and we simply take what would be disposed of anyway. The blood is still perfectly good when we get it."

"Do you transfuse it or do you just drink it?"

"We simply pour it into a glass and drink it. I like mine warm but most of my family prefer their blood chilled. Since we only get blood once a month, we make it something of a special occasion. Everyone dresses up in formal attire and Carmilla brings out the good crystal and white tablecloth. It's something like an elegant wine tasting."

"Edwin, have you ever killed a human?"

"No. I'm a vampire virgin."

"Have you thought about killing me?" Jezebella asked, obviously uncomfortable.

"Does that worry you?" I asked.

"It's just that in *Twilight* Bella never actually asked Edward if he had ever thought about killing her. The possibility would concern any normal person."

"I'm very dangerous Jezebella. I've already knocked you down twice, caused you two concussions, a sprained ankle, a broken middle finger, a black eye, and numerous bruises."

"Actually, I gave myself the black eye, but my finger still hurts," Jezebella said, extending her middle finger for me to see.

"You should always remember, Jezebella, that I am a very dangerous guy," I said, thinking of how intensely I yearned to ravage Jezebella and leave her dead, bloodless body in the woods.

"What about sunlight, Edwin? Does sunlight make you burst into flames or turn to dust like those vampires in the movies?"

"First of all, I would like to make clear that real vampires do not become effervescent, iridescent, sparkling, glittering, shimmering, flickering, opalescent, or prismatic in sunlight. In all of vampire history, there has never been a twinkling vampire. That nonsensical idea has set vampirism back at least two thousand years."

"Well, what does sunlight do to you?"

"Exposure to sunlight does have a very distressing consequence for vampires, but it does not harm us. The effect is extremely traumatic though."

"What happens, Edwin? How bad can it be?"

"I'm sorry, Jezebella. The subject is too upsetting to discuss."

"Please tell me, Edwin. I want to know everything about you."

"You wouldn't think of me in the same way."

"Nothing could ever change the way I feel about you, Edwin. I adore you. I'm obsessed with you. I live only for your approval."

"In that case, I promise that I'll tell you, but not tonight."

"I want to be a part of everything that you are, Edwin."

"This is wrong. It just isn't right. I may have to live with the problem, but I should not involve you in my wretched misery. I'm not good for you, Jezebella. Please understand that. I'm not a good person. I'm a dangerous guy. Please don't ever forget that."

"Edwin, I want to be with you, no matter how badly you treat me or how much you bruise me. I want to share your wretchedness. I'm nothing without you."

We were now parked in front of Jezebella's house. "Listen, Jezebella, now that you know about me and my family being vampires you must keep our secret. You can never reveal what you know to anyone."

"You can trust me. I would never tell anyone, Edwin. I promise."

"I believe you, Jezebella, but would you mind signing this legally binding nondisclosure agreement? I'm truly embarrassed to ask."

"Think nothing of it, Edwin. I'd do anything for you," Jezebella said, signing the document with a flourish.

"Thanks," I said, folding the papers into my pocket.

"It's dark. I really didn't mean to stay out so late," Jezebella said.

"I love the dark—the end of the day—the return of the night. It's the best time for us vampires to do our sneaking around," I said.

I stared wistfully into the night, contemplating my distant kinship with the vampires of old who came out only at night under the full moon. Now those were real vampires.

"Goodnight, Jezebella. I'll see you soon…. I mean, I'll see you at school tomorrow. Sleep well."

"I will. Goodnight, Edwin."

As I watched Jezebella walk to the front door, I could not help doubting the wisdom of having confessed my vampire secret to this human girl. Had I committed a colossal blunder, or would this story continue for three more books and end as the most overblown and mindless teen love story ever written?

Whatever the eventual outcome might be, about three things I was almost, more or less, absolutely positive. First, Jezebella was undeniably the most ordinary and average girl I had ever met. Second, there was a part of her, and I didn't know how stubbornly obsessive that part might be, that wanted me. And third, Jezebella's colorless personality dazzled me, and I was determined to make her my eternal vampire soul mate.

Chapter 7.
FAMILY DRAMA

After I brought Jezebella home, I went to tell my family that I had revealed the secret of our vampirism to Jezebella. In my own mind, I rationalized that there was no risk in trusting a fickle, brash, and immature human teenager with the secret of our existence. I reasoned that Jezebella would passionately protect our secret because of her obsession with me and out of gratitude for my romantic attentions. Predictably, my family was not of the same opinion. It turned out to be the most ridiculous argument we had ever had.

"Vampire family, I have an important announcement," I proclaimed solemnly.

"Everyone come into the living room. Edwin has an important announcement," Argyle said.

"This is so exciting," Carmilla said as she took a place on the sofa.

"Come on, Neville. Edwin has an announcement," Allison said as she and Neville slid down the stairway banister on skateboards.

"The last time Edwin made a family announcement was when he thought he was in love with that wanton harlot in Alaska," Rachel scoffed as she sat on the sofa beside Carmilla.

"Rachel, why are you nice to me in public but so heartlessly cruel to me here at home?" I asked with hurt feelings.

"Because at home we can be ourselves. It's the one place we don't have to hide our true feelings," Rachel sneered.

"You forget how sensitive and moody I am," I responded, making a mental note to shred her wardrobe.

"What is this big announcement?" Emrick asked as he entered the room and took a place beside Rachel.

"Well, to recap for everyone...."

"Not again Edwin!" The family groaned. "What now?"

"If I may continue without further interruption, my lust for Jezebella's tomato juice scent has been much more intense than any hunger, thirst, or craving for human blood that any of us has ever experienced, and I find myself helplessly drawn to Jezebella's pallid personality."

"Is there a point to be made in this century?" Rachel crabbily inquired.

"We know all of this. What are you trying to tell us?" Emrick asked in exasperation.

"My number was up with the first whiff of her scent. I knew immediately that I must have Jezebella and I resolved at that moment that she would be my girlfriend, my sweetheart, the object of my stalking. I observed that few boys at school paid attention to her after the first few days. She was virtually shunned, as if she were a naughty Amish girl caught in the barn with her bloomers down. I'm hopelessly smitten with this enigmatic girl whose no-frills personality is weirdly, bizarrely fascinating."

"OMG, Edwin!" Allison blurted out. "Would you please get to the point? Everyone already knows about your idiotic obsession with the human girl."

"Good grief, Edwin. Do you think we're all blind?" Neville asked.

"You're all missing the point. This is so much more than mere obsession. I must have Jezebella or my life will be pointless and empty. Life without Jezebella would be like Dracula without

Van Helsing, Luke Skywalker without Darth Vader, or Harry Potter without Voldemort. She gives meaning to my lonely, empty existence."

"That is so nice for you, Edwin. It warms my heart to see you less lonely," Carmilla said, smiling approvingly.

"Get on with it, Edwin," Argyle pleaded. "I'm growing old over here."

"Yes, please. Get on with it," Rachel implored.

"I've called everyone together to confess that I have betrayed your trust and quite possibly compromised the fictitious life that hides our true identity, by revealing to an impetuous and mercurial human teenager the true nature of our existence. I have told Jezebella Penguin that we are vampires."

For several interminable seconds stunned disbelief filled the room. My family was silent and unmoving, each frozen in their place, dumbfounded, dazed, and speechless. One by one, they looked at each other, trying to comprehend the enormity of my confession.

Argyle spoke first. "Edwin, do you understand the seriousness of what you have done? Carmilla and I have worked hard to establish an undercover life for our family. Finding such a charmingly bizarre town like Full Moon where we could blend in so well wasn't easy."

"Oh, Edwin, what have you done?" Carmilla whispered.

"How could you do this to us?" Rachel asked angrily.

"Our secret is safe with Jezebella. She won't tell anyone," I declared.

"How can you be so sure?" Neville asked.

"What makes you think you can trust her?" Allison added.

59

Joseph Veillon

"If not for my attention and affection, Jezebella would be forced to seek romance with the likes of Fig, Elliot, or Tyson. She would never betray my trust," I answered.

"Keeping our secret will be extremely difficult for Jezebella," Emrick said. "How could she not be tempted to tell someone about us? Just think how popular she would be at school if she exposed a coven of vampires living right here in Full Moon. Everyone would want to be her fake friend."

"The television talk shows would go wild. Leno, Ellen, and Letterman would stop at nothing to outwit each other and get the first interview with Jezebella. She could even sell the story to one of those illiterate tabloid rags," Allison declared. "That would be so degrading."

"She might even write a book about us," Rachel added.

"Please, not a fifth book," Neville groaned. "I couldn't take another one."

"Edwin, Jezebella is a seventeen year old girl. Adolescent humans are moody, temperamental, and unpredictable. And, human girls are not known for their ability or inclination to keep secrets. Trusting Jezebella with our secret was an unbelievably foolish thing to do," Carmilla admonished.

"This is not good. I don't like this at all, Edwin. You have put us in a very bad position," Rachel complained.

"Rachel is right, Edwin. You should not have told Jezebella about us without first consulting the family," Argyle stated rather sternly.

"How could you trust our secret to a human you've known for only six weeks?" Rachel scolded. "What you did was stupid."

"Edwin, do you honestly think you know anything about this girl?" Allison asked.

60

"You've spent five of the past six weeks not even talking to Jezebella. In fact, you've been pretending that she doesn't even exist," Rachel declared.

"I was not pretending that Jezebella doesn't exist."

"Okay, maybe you were pretending to pretend that Jezebella does not exist, but it seemed like you were actually pretending that she does not exist," Allison explained.

"The point is that you don't really know anything about Jezebella. You have confided our secret to a virtual stranger. How stupid, foolish, irrational, and thoughtless could you be?" Rachel asked.

"Edwin, what you did was appallingly irresponsible," Argyle declared.

"Words like idiot, moron, imbecile, half-wit, cretin, and feeble-minded come to mind." Rachel was enjoying herself immensely.

"We cannot simply trust Jezebella to do the right thing. She may not always be so taken with Edwin," Neville said.

"Edwin, what do you think will happen when Jezebella gets older?" Carmilla asked. "Humans, especially human females, are superficial and shallow enough that the age difference between you and Jezebella will be a huge issue. In fact, you already know that it will matter. Bella made it plain in those *Twilight* books."

"Edwin, Jezebella doesn't want to be older than you," Allison added.

"She won't be. I'm nearly 104 years old," I protested.

"In human terms you are still seventeen, Edwin, and you will always look seventeen," Allison went on. "Jezebella will be eighteen on her next birthday. This is already a problem."

"If you and Jezebella break up she may not feel obligated to keep our secret," Neville chimed in.

Joseph Veillon

"Book deal!" Rachel called out. "Somebody call Little and Brown."

"Things like that happen all the time," Allison added. "When people break up, their secrets and personal stuff get posted all over the internet. You haven't taken any compromising photographs, have you?"

"Even if we leave out all the rest, there is another major complication that we must consider," Argyle interjected. "What about the Sicilian Vultures?"

"Not the Sicilian Vultures!" Everyone whispered together in hushed horror as "Tubular Bells" suddenly began playing in the background.

"Edwin's revelation of our secret has violated the supreme law of the vampire world. He has dishonored the blood oath taken on the pilgrimage to Castle Dracula in Transylvania," Emrick announced in a solemn tone as he and everyone in the family crossed themselves thirteen times.

"Like the rest of us, he swore the vow in the gloomy shadows of Vlad Dracul's festering, mildewed tomb," Neville added.

"The Vultures will definitely come if they learn of Edwin's transgression," Argyle declared in a grave tone.

"The Vultures are so disagreeable and unpleasant," Rachel commented with a shudder. "They have such an unsophisticated fashion sense."

"The last time the Vultures visited they stayed a whole month," Carmilla complained. "They were loathsome, grubby, uncultured house guests. I thought they would never leave."

"It will be worse than that if they come again," Argyle asserted. "This time they will want Edwin, and they will bring the witch, Paine."

"Not Paine, the witch!" Everyone hissed in repugnance as the imaginary "Tubular Bells" continued to play.

"That tramp sorceress is even more shameless than Edwin's Alaskan floozy," Rachel observed.

"Would they really bring Paine?" Carmilla asked, almost in tears.

"That will be the Vulture's price for Edwin's indiscretion. His atonement will be to marry Paine," Argyle answered.

"No, not marry the witch!" The family objected in utter revulsion. The Vultures have been trying to marry off Paine for the past four hundred years, but there are few vampire misdeeds that justify such an ugly fate.

"Paine is rather beautiful though," Neville observed.

"True, but she's just such a witch," Rachel added.

"And there's that unpleasant thing that she does," Allison said.

"Yes, that thing," everyone agreed all at once in subdued voices.

"There is something we can do," I declared, suddenly remembering that I coveted and desired Jezebella to be my eternal soul mate. "We do have a way to solve this problem and avoid a visit by the Vultures."

"Yes, of course we do," Rachel agreed. "What is it?"

"I know exactly what you're thinking," Allison said quite excitedly.

"We need to work out how we're going to handle this," Carmilla said. "There will be much to prepare."

"We should do this soon," Emrick advised. "Full Moon is a world away from the Vultures, but they have an uncanny talent for sniffing things out."

Joseph Veillon

"This is a very serious issue and we all need to be together on this. We should put the matter to a family vote," Argyle declared.

Chapter 8.

AN INVITATION

Today began as a typical March morning in Full Moon, Washington—dismally cold and cloudy with a light rain. Now that I had disclosed my most intimate secret to her, I decided to surprise Jezebella and offer her a ride to school today. Arriving at her home on K Street, I noticed that vapors rising from the sewers had enveloped the neighborhood in a greenish, ghostly fog. I could almost swear that I saw ghoulish pirate zombies shambling through the mist.

Peering through the gauzy haze, it dawned on me that, in spite of the mist, even the most unobservant driver would easily see my car in the driveway, but I parked in the street just in case some clueless person might blindly back down the short driveway and hit my car parked in plain sight. Jezebella was just coming out of the house as I managed to park parallel to the curb on my fourth attempt. I was never very good at parking.

"Hello, Jezebella," I said. "Would you like a ride to school today?"

"Good morning, Edwin." Her voice betrayed no hint of nervousness at having learned that a family of vampires inhabited her town.

"Since I'm breaking all the rules now, I was wondering if you would like to ride to school with me this morning and let everyone jealously gossip about you."

"You want me to ride to school in your car?" she asked in disbelief.

"Yes, if you wouldn't be too embarrassed," I answered.

"No offence, but your car is an ancient relic held together with duct tape and super glue. Gnarly's lawnmower has more horsepower than your Yugo. Thanks, but I'll drive my 350 horsepower shiny new car that runs like a rocket. Why don't you ride with me?"

"That would be awesome!" I exclaimed, jumping at the chance to ride in Jezebella's new car.

"Here, Edwin. You'd better put on this bicycle helmet," she said.

Jezebella launched out of the driveway like a missile and was burning rubber toward school before I could fasten my seatbelt. The girl drove like a maniacal fiend, speeding through town as if pursued by a horde of shrieking demons. I would notice later that her personalized license plate quite fittingly reads *100MPH*.

"Edwin, is everything you told me last night the truth?"

"I should not have revealed such sensitive and compromising information, but everything I told you last night is absolutely true," I answered. "It was a mistake for me to tell you such a delicate secret."

"Maybe you should have thought of that sooner," Jezebella said quietly.

"What do you mean?" I asked.

"Because now you have all of this regret over foolishly telling your most intimate family secret to a flighty and impulsive girl like me."

"You think I regret revealing my deepest secret to a mere human that I've known for only six weeks?"

"You know virtually nothing about me," Jezebella reminded me. "Yes. I do think that you regret telling me your secret."

"You're wrong, Jezebella."

"I think you regret that you did not just let me ignorantly blather on about imaginary vampires and make myself look foolish, irrational, and crazy."

"You don't know anything. I do not regret revealing my family secret to an immature teenage girl that I hardly know."

"I can't help but think that while you are saying one thing, you are really trying to say something else, like you're at odds with yourself about what you truly want to say, as if you're conflicted about how you truly feel," Jezebella said. "After all, a lot of what you said throughout *Twilight* was ambiguous, vacillating, and indecisive."

"You're quite perceptive," I acknowledged.

We had arrived at school and by now had been sitting in the parking lot for several minutes. It was nearly time for our first class.

"We should go inside. I don't want to be late," Jezebella said.

"I'll walk you to class," I said as we pushed our way through a crowd of students who were admiring Jezebella's car, chattering and gawking at the car as if we were not even present. It was an interesting combination—the colorful, flamboyant red car and the pale, understated Jezebella.

It was raining by lunch. I met Jezebella in the hall and we walked into the cafeteria together. Everyone in the room immediately stopped what they were doing and ogled us as if we were a pair of naked mutant albino curiosities. Eyes popped wide open in disbelief, mouths dropped agape and people moved aside to make room for us as we walked through the curious throng. Angelica smiled knowingly and took our picture, while Fig looked stricken, as if he thought that Jezebella might be on my lunch menu.

"Everyone is staring at us," Jezebella whispered.

"Actually, they're admiring my unblemished perfection and appreciating how lucky you are to be in my company. Just stay close to me and bask in the glow of my resplendence."

Ejecting a couple of freshman students from their table, I deposited my books and proceeded to the food bar where I began dropping apples and trying to roll them off my shoe and into my hands. I finally got it on my thirteenth attempt.

"I'm just amazed at how you do that," Jezebella said as the entire cafeteria enthusiastically ignored me.

I then grabbed a tray and loaded it with pizza, yogurt, assorted fruit, oatmeal cookies, a root beer, and a warm tomato juice.

"Isn't there a special on bean and cheese burritos today?" Jezebella asked.

"Yes, but unless you want to spend the afternoon sitting in the bathroom you'll avoid the cafeteria burritos."

"Thanks for the tip," she said. "Edwin, I just noticed that your eyes are brown today. They were hazel. And, by the way, your family is staring at us."

"Actually, they're only staring at you," I replied, taking a bite of an apple and finding a worm wiggling at me as if waving hello.

"They look so serious. Is anything wrong?"

"They're just being themselves. Don't worry about it." I gave a low growl and they all immediately changed their expressions. "See, now they're smiling and waving."

"Seeing Emrick reminds me of your expedition last weekend. Did he find any butterflies?"

"We had a great time. Emrick found a very rare solid black butterfly with little red hearts on its wings. He was very excited."

68

"I heard that the area where you and Emrick went butterfly hunting is bear country. Have you ever hunted bears?"

"The black bears in Washington are not really very aggressive. They would not be much of a challenge if we did hunt them."

"Would the bears be more dangerous in the spring when they were just coming out of hibernation?" Jezebella asked. "I read that bears were more bad-tempered during that time."

"You would be grumpy too if you had starved all winter. But in a fight the bear would be handicapped by weakness from all those months of hibernation."

"Nothing more fun than fighting a disabled bear," Jezebella mocked. "I bet that grizzly bears would be more dangerous."

"Any vampire hunting grizzly bears in this state would go hungry. There are almost no grizzly bears left in the state of Washington and grizzly sightings are actually quite rare. In fact, grizzly bears are a threatened species under the Endangered Species Act and it would be both illegal and ecologically irresponsible to hunt grizzlies in Washington."

"I certainly would not want Gnarly to arrest you for illegal bear hunting."

"We believe in doing our part for the environment," I said.

At that moment the bell rang and it was time once again for biology. I hated to interrupt my conversation with Jezebella, but today we were watching a film on the mating habits of penguins and I didn't want to miss anything. It wasn't until after school that I was able to talk with Jezebella again.

"Hello, Jezebella. How was your afternoon?" I asked, catching up with her in the parking lot.

"Hey, Edwin. You won't believe what happened in gym today."

"What happened?" I asked.

"I was walking past Coach Hardwicke by the pool and all of a sudden she screamed and jumped into the water with all of her clothes still on."

"You're kidding!" I exclaimed.

"No. She just jumped in and started cursing and shaking her fist in the air. It was really bizarre. By the way, what are you doing here?"

"You're my ride today, remember?"

"Oh. Are you sure? I guess I forgot," she said, unlocking the car.

"Jezebella, we need to talk," I said as I eased into the front passenger seat and put on the bicycle helmet. "I need to know that you're not freaked out about having a family of vampires in the neighborhood."

"No. You're membership in the undead society doesn't bother me. But you're really asking if I'm going to tell anyone, aren't you?" Jezebella asked as she floored the accelerator and roared out of the parking lot.

"Yes, I am!" I shouted as I braced myself and pulled the seatbelt tighter.

"Edwin, I promised that I would never reveal your secret. I may be a bit scatterbrained and something of an airhead, but I signed your nondisclosure agreement and I won't break my promise. I even wrote this reminder on my arm during last period."

Jezebella held out her arm so I could read the message— DO NOT TELL ANYONE THAT EDWIN DULLEN IS A VAMPIRE.

"And what do you think, now that you've had some time to think about what you've learned?"

70

"There are a lot of weird things going on around Full Moon. We may as well have vampires too. Does your family know that you told me their secret?"

"Yes. I told them last night after I brought you home."

"Edwin, even I think that you were foolish to tell me your family secret. How did they react?"

"The prevailing opinion is that it was a stupid thing to do. Rachel called me a half-wit and several other hurtful names. Everyone is so fixated on the idea that I don't know anything about you. I don't understand it."

"I have to agree with them on that point, Edwin."

"But that is how it was written in *Twilight*," I protested.

"Edwin, it may have been written that way but that doesn't make it smart."

"Again, you're very perceptive. I guess that I'm just trying to rationalize making such an idiotic goof."

"That's enough about you, Edwin. How does your family feel about me?"

"They're confused. They don't understand why I would choose you over more popular and beautiful girls like Selene or Miriam."

"I don't understand that either, Edwin. I'm entirely ordinary and plain, and you're so totally gorgeous and perfect."

"You certainly do see things clearly, Jezebella."

We had arrived at Jezebella's house and were now parked in the driveway. It felt good to take off the bike helmet, but my hands and knees were still trembling from the ride.

"Edwin, your family doesn't hate me, do they?"

"They just don't understand why I can't stay away from you."

"But, it's not just you, Edwin. I'm chasing you just as much as you're chasing me. I hope they don't hate me."

"They don't hate you. Quite the contrary, they would like to offer you an invitation."

"Oh, good, that means they must really like me. Is it a party?"

"Jezebella, I…. we would like you to join our family."

"Join your family? I'm a little confused, Edwin. I already have a family."

"I know, but we thought that you might like to be a part of our family too."

"You want me to have two families? Wow! You must really like me a lot. But I don't even know your family, Edwin. I haven't met any of them."

"Don't worry about that, Jezebella. You would have lots of time to get to know them."

"But, Edwin, they might not like me."

"Jezebella, we've already voted and we want you to become a vampire and join our family."

"You want me to be a vampire?" she asked in disbelief.

"Yes. Just think, you could be as beautiful, perfect, and cool as all of us. The kids at school would be totally jealous and resentful of you. It's a fine feeling to know that everyone else feels inferior to you."

"Edwin, I'm totally down with hanging out with you, and I would love to meet your family, but I don't want to be a vampire."

"Why not?" I asked, surprised that anyone would turn down an opportunity for eternal beauty and perfection.

"Well, your skin is even more anemic looking than mine, and you have those dark circles under your eyes all the time. And, your eyes keep changing colors. It just looks weird."

"But all of that is part of the perfection, Jezebella. You'll get used to it, eventually."

"That's not all, Edwin. I could never drink blood. It's gross. I know you say it tastes like tomato juice, but I really don't like tomato juice. And what about the smell? I'm sorry, but you know that you have that mausoleum aroma."

"I'm sorry, Jezebella. You know that I can't help it. Besides, it would be several years before you really started to smell."

"Edwin, I just couldn't handle having that kind of body odor. I'm obsessively self-conscious about just having bad breath."

"You would eventually get used to it, Jezebella. It really is a small price to pay for the perks of vampire life."

"Edwin, you've had almost ninety years to think about and accept the reality of being a vampire, but you don't understand what you're asking."

"But I do, Jezebella. Right now, every second of every minute of every hour of each and every day, you are getting older and older."

"Thank you for bringing that to my attention, Edwin. A reminder of the relentless progression of time to arthritic and forgetful old age is just what I needed."

"That is exactly my point, Jezebella. You would never age if you were a vampire. You would always look young and ordinary. We would both be seventeen forever."

"Edwin, it isn't supposed to be that way. You're actually over one hundred years old and it just isn't right for someone with your maturity to be so interested in someone my age. It's kind of creepy."

"I understand, Jezebella. It's okay. Maybe you just aren't ready. It doesn't have to be right now, but then again, there's no reason that it shouldn't be now."

"I can think of several. Haven't you been listening to me?"

"Of course I have, but I'm not letting this go," I answered.

"Okay, Edwin, but I hope you enjoy disappointment."

"Don't be difficult, Jezebella. You know, you could just thank me," I said, exasperated with Jezebella's stubbornness.

"Don't be so dramatic, Edwin. Do you want to meet here and ride to school with me again tomorrow?" Jezebella asked after scowling at me in silence for several seconds.

"That would be great," I said as we got out of the car. I noticed the lady next door standing on her porch with a cat held protectively in her arms. She gave us a very unfriendly look.

"That's Mrs. Swan. Her cat ran away and she just got a new one," Jezebella explained.

"Oh. I'll see you tonight…. I mean tomorrow morning," I said.

"Great. I'll see you tomorrow," Jezebella said, heading for the front door as I walked to my own car.

Chapter 9.

QUESTIONS

I was at Jezebella's house Thursday morning as soon as Gnarly left for work. It was colder than yesterday and continual rain had made the pavement slippery. Jezebella came bounding out of the house, raised her arm to wave and straightaway slipped on the icy walkway, landing on her butt with her feet splayed out in front of her.

"Are you okay?" I asked as I stood by and patiently waited for her to get up. "Did you hurt yourself?"

"I'm fine. I'm not usually so inept."

"Actually, you are."

"I'm such an uncoordinated klutz," Jezebella sighed.

"You know, you would be totally graceful and coordinated if you were a vampire," I observed.

"Forget about it, Edwin. It's not going to happen."

I carried Jezebella's book bag to her car and opened the door for her. She jumped in and started the car, revving the engine as I walked around to my side. We catapulted into the street like an F-16 fighter jet. Jezebella loved speed and we flew through town like a flaming meteor. The wild ride to school was mercifully short and I needed the barf bag only once. We roared into the parking lot and skidded neatly into a parking space created when the car knocked a bicycle rack out of the way. Mid-semester exams were being given today and we would not have time to talk much during the school day. I was already looking forward to lunch.

Joseph Veillon

"I'll see you later," I said as I got out of the car. "Good luck on your exams."

"Thanks. I'll see you later," she replied as we made our way into the building. "Good luck on your exams, Edwin."

The morning passed uneventfully. Since I had been through high school and college so many times, my exams were no challenge at all and I was always the first to finish. I love how that makes everyone jealous and resentful of me. I was already seated in the cafeteria when Jezebella arrived and I waved her over to my table.

"Hello," I said. "How have your exams been so far?"

"Math and English were brutal," Jezebella replied. "Numbers and words are so tricky for me."

"How was gym? You didn't push anyone into the pool today, did you?"

"I did not push Coach Hardwicke into the pool. She just happened to fall in as I was passing. It's not my fault," Jezebella answered quite defensively.

"Okay. Relax. I almost believe you. Have a root beer and an oatmeal cookie," I offered, pushing my tray toward her.

"Thanks, I *am* hungry. By the way, I've decided to go out for sports."

"Sports, really?"

"Yes, I joined the volleyball team."

"That's awesome, Jezebella. I heard that you have a mean spike."

"I'm really excited to make the team. They wouldn't let me play anything at my school in Phoenix."

"Congratulations and good luck," I said. "Jezebella, not to change the subject, but I've been meaning to ask if you had any boyfriends when you lived in Phoenix?"

"Only one, and for just a short time. His name was James."

"Interesting. Do you have a favorite color?"

"I like gray because gray is the color of the sky here and it matches my personality and customary mood. Green is nice too, because it's the color of that cool squashy moss that covers everything around Full Moon. I love walking barefoot in that stuff and feeling it squish between my toes."

"What's the last good movie you've seen?"

"I saw *Vampires Suck* a few weeks ago."

"I saw that movie too. It was really funny," I replied. "The disco scene was hilarious."

"Do you like plants?" I inquired.

"I brought a cactus from Phoenix, but it died. I'm thinking of planting a cactus garden though."

"You should consider planting wolfsbane," I suggested.

"Isn't wolfsbane a werewolf repellant?"

"Yes. I recommend that you plant lots of it all around your house."

"Okay. I'll consider that," Jezebella replied with a puzzled look on her face.

"Do you have any pets?"

"When I lived in Roswell I had a pet tarantula, but it died. In Phoenix, I had a goldfish and a hamster, but they died too. I also once had an ant farm, but the ants escaped. I adopted a puppy from the animal shelter, but it ran away. After that, I got an iguana, but someone stole it. After the iguana I got a cat, but it disappeared after a Chinese restaurant opened in our neighborhood."

"That's too bad. Maybe you should get a parrot."

"Actually, I did have a parrot once."

"Let me guess – it flew away."

Joseph Veillon

"No. My mom made me give it away because it talked with such vulgar language. We found out that some girls who worked in a bordello had once owned the parrot. That bird knew a lot of very dirty words."

"Are you going to get another pet?" I asked.

"It would be cool to have a pet wolf. I could name it Jake."

"Just make sure your wolf gets its shots," I advised.

The bell rang and people began leaving the cafeteria for their next exam. I had several more questions for Jezebella and I only grudgingly agreed to go to class. I could hardly wait for the end of the day.

"Jezebella, would you like to get a coffee with me after school today?" I asked, hopefully.

"Sure Edwin. That would be great. Meet me at my car after your Spanish exam."

I was anxious to talk more with Jezebella and the rest of the day passed much too slowly, as if time was standing still, but then I noticed that my watch had stopped. When school finally ended, I met Jezebella in the parking lot and we zoomed off to the café next door to the town library. We parked in front and went inside, taking a table with a choice view of Full Moon Avenue. I noticed a new waitress who soon came to take our order.

"Hello. I'm Kristen. Can I take your order?"

"I'd like a hazelnut coffee please," Jezebella said.

"I'll have a glass of warm tomato juice please," I added.

"One hazelnut coffee and one warm tomato juice coming right up. Will there be anything else?" Kristen asked.

"I'd also like an oatmeal cookie," Jezebella said.

"Great. I'll be right back with that," Kristen replied. I couldn't help but notice that her eyes lingered on Jezebella as she slowly turned to walk away.

78

"What's your favorite food, Jezebella?"

"I could live on pizza and chicken nuggets. I also like oatmeal cookies and banana pudding. Actually, I *love* banana pudding."

"Do you have any hobbies?"

"No. Apart from obsessing over you, I'm very indifferent and uninvolved. I don't do anything interesting. I'm actually pretty boring. However, I do like to cook. I always have frozen pizza, a microwave dinner, or fish sticks ready for Gnarly when he gets home from work."

"What do you do for fun?"

"My only real passion is dirty dancing. I even have some videos on YouTube."

"Do you have a favorite author?" I asked.

"I love J.K. Rowling's *Harry Potter* books," Jezebella replied.

"J.K. Rowling is a terrific writer. *Harry Potter* is amazing," I agreed.

"Better than amazing. *Harry Potter* is so much more well written than that bogus teen romance we got stuck in," Jezebella added.

"And, *Harry Potter* is a lot more interesting and fun to read," I said. "It has wizards, witches, magic, and adventure. All we had was a sparkling vampire."

"Harry and his friends are all such amazingly positive role models," Jezebella remarked. "Nobody criticizes their values."

"I know. If we had been in *Harry Potter* we could have been like that instead of being so shallow and disappointing," I said.

"And, in *Harry Potter* the female characters were treated with respect," Jezebella said, looking me right in the eye as she spoke. "Those girls were strong, intelligent characters. I wish I could have been like them."

"It would have been so totally awesome to be one of J.K. Rowling's characters," I said.

"Yeah, those kids really lucked out," Jezebella agreed.

"Do you like Stephen King?" I asked.

"Stephen King is an awesome writer. *Salem's Lot* is unquestionably the best vampire novel I've ever read," Jezebella answered.

"Now *that* is a vampire story," I agreed. "No one writes about vampires like Stephen King."

"*Salem's Lot* scared the bejesus out of me. I had to sleep with the lights on for months after reading that book," Jezebella added. "I was afraid a vampire would come into my room and bite me while I was sleeping."

"What's the best place you've ever been on vacation?" I asked.

"I've never been on a real vacation," Jezebella replied.

At that moment Kristen returned with our drinks. She placed my tomato juice on the table in front of me and did the same with Jezebella's coffee and oatmeal cookie.

"Here you go. Let me know if you need anything else," she said, winking at Jezebella.

"Thanks," Jezebella and I both said.

"Edwin, is that waitress flirting with me?"

"Yes. I think she likes you."

"I guess I'm just irresistible," Jezebella answered, giving me a coy smile and eyeing Kristen as she walked away.

"If you could go anywhere at all on vacation, where would you want to go?" I asked.

"It would be totally awesome to visit the Wizarding World of Harry Potter at that theme park in Florida," Jezebella replied. "Why are you asking me all of these questions?"

"Since I've been so meanly criticized for revealing my family's vampirism to someone that I barely know, I decided that I should learn more about you."

"Oh, okay. That's cool. You've got your work cut out for you, though. I don't even know myself very well."

"Then perhaps you'll take this do-it-yourself home edition personality test. Please have it back to me tomorrow."

"I don't know, Edwin. I don't really have much of an identity apart from my obsession with you. Say, your eyes were brown. Now they're amber. I've never known anyone whose eyes change color like that."

"Jezebella, do you have plans for Saturday?" I asked, ignoring her comment.

"No. As usual, I'm not doing anything. I'll just be staying home, not going to the dance, available for anyone who might want to call or visit," she said, giving me an inviting wink and lightly running her finger across my hand.

"Will Gnarly be home?"

"No. Gnarly and his deputies will be in the woods all weekend looking for rogue wolves," she answered, giving me another wink and rubbing her foot on my leg under the table.

"Would you like to go on an outing in the woods with me? I'd like to show you something. We could make it a picnic."

"Sure, Edwin. That sounds like fun."

"Great. I'll see you Saturday morning."

"Aren't you going to be in school tomorrow?"

"No. My family is going to Seattle for a meeting of our Vampires Anonymous support group. There's also a computer store in Seattle that I want to visit. Would you like another hazelnut coffee?"

"No. I should get home and put some fish sticks in the oven. Gnarly will be home soon. I also want to review my biology report. Our papers are due tomorrow, remember?"

"I saw you in the school library earlier. Were you doing some last minute research for your report?" I asked.

"Research? No way," Jezebella retorted. "I just wrote down some random stuff that I made up, but I didn't actually research anything."

I left money on the table for our drinks and a nickel tip as we got up to leave. Kristen smiled and gave Jezebella a little wave from the front counter as we walked outside. We got into Jezebella's car and were at her house in mere minutes.

"I'll see you tonight…. I mean Saturday morning," I said. "It'll be fun."

"Okay, Edwin. I'll see you Saturday."

Chapter 10.
SKINNY-DIPPING

Saturday morning dawned with a gloomily overcast sky, but Barbra, the ZOMB TV weather girl, was predicting ten minutes of sunshine for midday and rain was not expected until late afternoon. It would be a perfect day for our outing. My anxiety over spending the day with Jezebella had caused me to sleep fitfully and I had dreamed vividly of Paine and the Vultures coming for me. I spent a full four hours grooming my hair, brushing, flossing, whitening my teeth, and scrubbing with Vlad's Vampire Body Wash and Odor Control to subdue my cadaverous undead stench. I finished by slathering on several bottles of sunscreen and then splashing Old Spice cologne over my entire body.

I dressed myself in an anxious frenzy, donning brown suede-leather hiking shoes, faded denim jeans, a black long-sleeved shirt, and a Full Moon High School sweatshirt. Checking my look in the mirror, the black shirt contrasted perfectly with the pink sweatshirt.... *whoa! Pink?* In my hurry, I had mistakenly grabbed one of Allison's sweatshirts. Exchanging the girlie pink thing for my own black Full Moon High School sweatshirt, I again checked myself in the mirror. I looked good, like a model or even a modern-day Greek god. After a breakfast of warm tomato juice and croissants dripping with strawberry jam, I was ready for Jezebella Penguin.

I arrived at Jezebella's house exactly five seconds after Gnarly left for work. She must have been watching for me because she was at the front door and fumbling to get it open before

I had a chance to knock. Jezebella struggled with the simple lock and I was eventually forced to use my lock picking skills to get inside the house. Jezebella's mind was undoubtedly still muddled by her gratuitous use of cold medicine the previous night. A minor taking unnecessary cold medicine to induce sleep—now *that* is truly setting a bad example for impressionable adolescents.

"Good morning," I said, shuddering with muffled laughter in spite of a heroic attempt to suppress my considerable amusement.

"What are you laughing at—are you laughing at me?" Jezebella asked, apparently realizing at that very instant that she had not finished dressing and was not wearing pants. She turned and bolted like greased lightning up the stairs, her entire body flushed in embarrassment, leaving me at the door with an illicit image of her yellow undies decorated with little blue bumblebees. Several long minutes passed before Jezebella came back down the stairs.

"Don't say a word Edwin. Just don't say anything," she commanded. "If this had not been written into *Twilight* we would not have had to spoof it and I would have been spared this undignified humiliation."

"I agree. The way your character was written makes you an especially attractive target for literary mockery and criticism."

"Thanks, Edwin. I feel so much better now. You know, you deserve your fair share of ridicule as well."

"I hardly think so. My character was written as beautiful and perfect. In the *Twilight* book it says so 165 times, more or less."

"Who better to mock than an angst-ridden, narcissistic, vampire with a conflicted self-image? You can't even make up your mind about whether or not you want to kill me."

"I could remedy that particular issue right now if you wish," I offered.

"Not so fast fang boy. We have more stuff to make fun of, critique, and spoof. This parody isn't over yet. Let's get going."

"Would you like to take my car today, Jezebella?"

"Sure. I'll ride in the silver turtle. We have all day."

I opened the passenger door and helped Jezebella into the car, and then went around and got into the driver's seat. The Yugo mercifully started on the first try and thankfully accelerated without the usual coughing, sputtering, and gagging of the feeble engine. Ignoring her taunts about needing to speed up if we were going to make it out of town before dark, I eased my way through Jezebella's neighborhood to South Full Moon Avenue, turned right, and drove past the pizza shop and Lost Expedition Outfitters, past the Timber Museum, the airport, and Straker's Mortuary at the edge of town, taking Highway 101 southward out of Full Moon.

"Where are we going, Edwin?"

"About twenty-seven miles or so from Full Moon, Highway 101 reaches the ocean near Ruby Beach, and just a little farther down the coast there's an abandoned park service road that runs into the forest."

"We're going down some old abandoned road into the forest?" Jezebella asked skeptically.

"It's an unused road that was closed years ago. We'll follow it a few miles and then make a short hike into the woods."

"Oh, good. I love hiking. In fact, at my school in Phoenix, we had to do a community service project and for my project I paired up with some senior citizens and took them hiking around the mall. I got really good at it. Where exactly are we going on this hike?"

"I have a special place that I want you to see."

"A special place? What is it, Edwin?"

"You'll see soon enough," I replied. "Jezebella, there seems to be a convoy of cars following us," I said, observing in the rear-view mirror a line of several vehicles that had followed us from Full Moon.

"That's my entourage," Jezebella replied.

"Your entourage?"

"Yes. Just a few people I brought along to make sure there would be no question about me getting back home alive—Angelica, Elliot, Selene, Miriam, Salem, Victoria, and a few others. I also took out a front page notice in the Full Moon Forum, posted our outing on my Facebook page, and left a note with my lawyer."

"So, everyone knows you're with me?"

"Yeah, pretty much."

"Well, that's very helpful, Jezebella. I guess now I'll have to bring you back," I said jokingly.

"What did you expect, Edwin? After all, you *are* a vampire and you keep telling me how dangerous you are. I'm not suicidal, except maybe for that little cliff jumping affair and that motorcycle episode in New Moon. Oh, and in the *Twilight* movie I walked into the woods all alone to confront you about being a vampire. Anyway, I wouldn't want you to get into trouble."

"You're worried about the trouble that *I* would be in if *you* disappeared?" I asked, a little confused.

"Of course, Edwin. If you were in trouble it would mean that I was dead." I certainly could not argue with Jezebella's logic.

After about thirty minutes we reached the Ruby Beach parking area where Highway 101 turns south and parallels the rocky shore and narrow beaches of the coastline. We passed Destruction Island and a few minutes farther down the coast we came to the old park service road and turned left into the forest. Long neglected and with vegetation encroaching close along both sides, the road was now hardly more than a thin trail winding through the dark, primordial woods.

"You know, this forest is really dark and spooky," Jezebella remarked.

"Don't worry. I won't let the boogeyman get you."

"Edwin, isn't there a scary ghost story about these woods?"

"I wasn't going to mention it, but a few years ago a girl from Full Moon named Heather Blair disappeared in the woods and was never found. Some hikers found her video camera at an old Indian burial site. According to the police, the footage looked like the camera had been recording as something chased Heather Blair through the woods."

"And she was never found?"

"Heather Blair vanished without a trace."

"Now that is really creepy. I think I've heard enough of your ghost story. How much farther is it to this special place of yours?"

"Actually, we're almost there," I said as I slowed to a stop. "From here we have just a little hike, which reminds me, those tennis shoes you're wearing won't do for hiking through these woods. I brought you a pair of proper hiking shoes."

I produced the hiking shoes from the back of my car and gave them to Jezebella. I pulled out my backpack and checked my supplies while she changed shoes.

"What's in the backpack?" Jezebella asked.

"Just some energy bars, water, tomato juice, root beer, matches, flashlights, an emergency personal locator beacon, a GPS receiver, two space blankets, toilet paper, and a couple of rain jackets and extra socks. One should always be prepared when hiking in the woods."

"You've thought of everything," Jezebella said.

"Follow me," I said as I stepped from the road into the trees. "Stay close to me."

"Don't worry about me. I'm an excellent hiker. I trained at the mall."

"Actually, I was thinking about what happened to Heather Blair."

"Don't scare me!"

Jezebella and I chattered almost nonstop as we hiked. What little light that was available was filtered by the overcast sky and the thickness of the forest overhead and Jezebella remarked several times on the spooky shadows. The trail was old and unused and in many places we had to negotiate a labyrinth of rocks, roots, vines, briars, deadfalls, and other obstacles that threatened to snare the unwary or the uncoordinated. Incredibly, after hiking unscathed over the most dangerous three miles of trail, Jezebella tripped over her own feet and nearly broke an ankle on a clear, flat, smooth stretch of trail. I took her by the hand and picked her up to help her over the obstructions at every opportunity, never wanting to let go of her. I tried not to look at her too much, but it was difficult not to focus on her beautiful plainness.

"Are we close, Edwin? We've been hiking for ages. What is that roaring sound up ahead?"

"We're almost there now."

"What is it, Edwin? What's making that noise?"

"It's my waterfall," I said, as the thick vegetation of the forest opened onto a tiny, perfectly square meadow full of brightly colored flowers, revealing a magnificent waterfall gushing from the precipice forty feet above us and cascading over the granite rock face into a small pool at the base of a cliff on the far side of the meadow.

"Wow! This is so way cool! This is the most amazing place I have ever seen in all my seventeen years."

"I knew you would like it."

"I love it! It's…. magical. How did you find this place?"

"There are several popular waterfalls in the area. I was hiking in the woods one day, looking for a waterfall too isolated and out-of-the-way for tourists, when I got lost for two days and discovered this place. No one else knows about it."

"Now that we're here Edwin, you promised to tell me what happens to you in the sunlight."

"According to the weather forecast we have thirty minutes before the sun comes out. Let's go for a swim."

"I didn't bring a swim suit," Jezebella protested.

"I don't have one either."

"You mean…. go skinny-dipping?" she said in mock disbelief.

"Or, we could just lay here among the flowers in the meadow," I offered.

"No way. Who wants to lay around in a meadow? Let's go swimming," Jezebella decided. "Turn around while I undress and get into the water."

"I won't look," I promised.

"Don't you peek at me," Jezebella said.

I turned my back to Jezebella and slowly removed my clothes, resisting a devilish yearning to steal a glimpse as she disrobed. When I heard Jezebella splash into the water I turned and dived in behind her, delighted to see her yellow undies with the blue bumblebees resting on top of her neatly folded jeans and sweater. I quickly swam over to her.

"You were peeking at me," I said.

"You said that *you* wouldn't look," Jezebella replied. "But I never promised that I wouldn't look."

We spent several minutes playfully splashing each other under the icy shower of the waterfall. I pulled Jezebella close and nervously kissed her lips, unsure of what her reaction would be. She surprised me completely by enthusiastically mashing her lusciously plain body snugly against me and passionately returning my kiss.

"You have no idea how that feels," I sighed after several moments.

"You obviously still have some deep human instincts," Jezebella observed.

"What do you mean?"

"Well, at least one part of you seems to be thoroughly human."

"I do still have certain human desires and I sometimes hunger for more than blood. Never forget that I crave more than your company."

"To say that it was very obvious right now would be an understatement," Jezebella replied with a wide grin.

"Oops," I replied before pressing my mouth to hers once again.

After several more minutes of kissing we finally untangled our tongues and reluctantly pulled our lips apart. What I could see of Jezebella's body was flushed quite red and her breath was now coming in short, passionate gasps. I feared that she might swoon or have an episode of heart palpitations. We timidly laughed at our unsophisticated awkwardness and naïve self-consciousness, but we each refused to surrender our skintight embrace of the other.

"Edwin, would you like a taste?" Jezebella asked.

"A taste? Of your blood, seriously?" I asked, not quite believing what I had just heard. This was unbelievable – beyond my most fervent hope and wildest fantasy.

"You could prick my finger and have a little taste," Jezebella offered, rubbing a finger lightly over my lips and then easing it into my mouth.

I closed my mouth around Jezebella's finger and sucked on it gently, savoring her mouthwatering essence. Jezebella moaned softly, wrapped her legs tightly around me, and then leaned her head down and gave me a long kiss on the neck. I was desperate to bite Jezebella's finger and taste her sweet blood, but my inner vampire was screaming for release and I did not know if I would be able to stop myself with only one small taste. My lust for Jezebella's blood was every bit as powerful as my nearly out of control carnal desire.

"Oh, Edwin," Jezebella whimpered. "You're making me crazy. You can't imagine what you're doing to me."

"Probably something like what you're doing to me," I replied after slipping her finger out of my mouth. "You are such a naughty temptress."

"Please don't stop, Edwin," Jezebella begged, caressing my lips with her finger. "I want you to taste my blood."

"Jezebella, as much as I want you, I don't know if this is a good idea."

Then, at that inopportune, ill-timed, intrusive, and most inconvenient moment, the pitiless and unfeeling sun peered through the gray clouds and cruelly shone its resplendent golden radiance onto us as we reveled in our idyllic ecstasy. The merciless sunbeams washed over me like sadistic ogres bent on my total mortification, disgrace, shame, and degradation and their touch had an immediate and dramatic effect.

The mortifying transformation seemed to happen in slow motion and go on forever, although the whole ugly process took only seconds. The wave of hideous disfigurement washed over me like the shadow of some unholy demon risen up from the depths of hell. I felt like my body was on fire, burning with a heat so intense that I feared the vitreous fluid of my eyeballs would boil and cause the orbs to burst forth from their sockets. My skin turned a revolting, cadaverous shade of green dappled with blood-tinged patches of black and gray colored putrefaction, while oozing ulcers and pus-filled boils erupted alongside gangrenous lesions on nearly every exposed surface of my formerly unblemished skin. My teeth, holding in my swollen, purplish tongue, sharpened and elongated into cavity-pocked fangs stained brownish-yellow with age, while my hair stood out from my head as if the atmosphere was charged with static electricity.

"Oh my God, Edwin!" Jezebella cried as she swam backwards away from me in utter shock and revulsion, as if she had just seen a naked 104-year-old man appear before her eyes. "Oh my God! What are you?" She choked out the question through a flood of tears.

"Don't be afraid, Jezebella. Please don't be afraid of me," I pleaded.

"I'm ready to get out of the water now," she said rather shakily as she swam to the spot where we had left our clothes.

"There are two towels in my backpack," I called to her.

"Just turn around and don't look until I say you can."

The sun had already vanished again behind dark gray clouds by the time Jezebella reached the edge of the pond, and

I transformed back into a beautiful and perfect vampire just as quickly as the horrid metamorphosis had overtaken me. I turned and swam toward Jezebella, who by now had wrapped herself in a towel and was sitting in the grass watching me with a look of amazement on her face.

"Turn around so I can come out," I said.

"Not a chance," she answered with a wide grin, her tears having vanished. "Now that I've seen your inner beast I'll have even more appreciation for your beauty."

"At least throw me a towel."

"Come and get it," she taunted.

I endured the several seconds of embarrassment that it took to climb from the water and wrap the towel around my body, and then sat in the grass next to Jezebella, who had scrutinized me quite closely the whole time.

"I'm so ashamed, Jezebella. This is humiliating."

"Don't worry Edwin. That beastly mutation thing was definitely shocking, but I know you can't help it. At least you didn't sparkle. However, I wish that we had not been engaged in an intimate embrace at the time."

"I'm really very sorry, Jezebella. I truly don't want to be a monster."

"Edwin, I don't care what you are. I'm not judgmental. I'll overlook anything that stands in the way of being with you."

Jezebella and I lay in the grass without talking for several minutes, allowing the embarrassment of the moment to pass. A dragonfly buzzed near me and so I used my vampire ability to still my body and remain motionless in order to lure it close. When the dragonfly settled onto a blade of grass between us, I quickly grabbed it and plucked off its wings and its head, much to Jezebella's horror. I imagined that she must have been thinking of the danger she could be in at the moment.

"I'm the most dangerous predator in the world," I bragged, picking up a dead one-inch-thick branch from the ground and snapping it in half. "Are you afraid?"

"I guess I might be if I were a dragonfly or a dried-out twig," Jezebella responded somewhat warily.

"Don't be frightened," I said in my most soothing and seductive voice. "I simply had a future serial killer moment. I don't know what came over me. Besides, you could probably outrun me or even fight me off. I'm not very athletic."

"Does anything ever scare you, Edwin?"

"I was once mobbed by a pack of Twilight Moms. That was even more terrifying than those Twilighters in Devil's Harbor."

"Is that how you got that scar on your shoulder?"

"No. A crazed girl named Buffy attacked me a few years ago. She stabbed me with a dagger."

"I can't imagine why anyone would do that," Jezebella mocked. "I'm hungry. What kind of food did you bring?"

"Six flavors of energy bars," I answered.

"Energy bars? Is that all? You brought energy bars for our picnic?" Jezebella's tone sounded as if she was accusing me of some heinous crime.

I retrieved the energy bars from my backpack and laid them on a small tablecloth for Jezebella to inspect. "They really are quite good," I offered.

"I'll have one of those peanut butter bars and a root beer, if you please," Jezebella said.

We lay next to each other among the flowers, munching our energy bars and enjoying the gray overcast of the sky, imagining a romantic Carter Burwell lullaby playing just for us.

"Edwin, why are your lips trembling like that? Are you singing to yourself?"

"No. I'm chanting a Tibetan prayer of thanks."

"Why?"

"Your towel is open."

"You're a pervert," Jezebella said, pulling the towel more tightly around her body and unconsciously curling her toes deeper into the grass.

"From now on I will be a perfect gentleman," I promised with my fingers crossed behind my back.

"Edwin, tell me what happened that day at school when we first met. Your behavior was very strange."

"Vampires are very sensitive to the smell of humans, which can sometimes throw our bodies into a macabre dance of perverse contortions and ghoulish frenzies as we fight our natural urge to kill you and drink your blood."

"There were several other people in class, Edwin. Why did you react that way only to me?"

"Consider an addict. If you put a sex addict in a room with an unkempt, unwashed person of dubious medical history, even an addict with an insatiable hunger for carnal gratification and libidinal indulgence could abstain. However, if you hooked him up with a hot young actress from the movie *Twilight*, well…. who could possibly resist?"

"What?" Jezebella gave me a puzzled look, apparently not understanding my explanation.

"Think of it this way," I said. "If you offered boiled broccoli to a hungry man, he might eat it, but he wouldn't like it very much. But, if you offered him chocolate covered strawberries with whipped cream, he would undoubtedly devour it with great pleasure."

"So, you're saying that you lust after me as if I were covered with chocolate, strawberries, and whipped cream. I'm your brand of dessert."

"You are exactly my brand of dessert."

"Speaking of scent Edwin, that disgusting stench oozing off of you that first day nearly gagged me. In that interminable fifty minutes of class, I must have thought of at least ninety-nine different ways to get away from your reeking stench, but all of the other seats in class were taken and I was fresh out of reasons to go see the school nurse."

"The smell was definitely a complication. There is little I can do to hide the rotting stink from nearly eighty-seven years of gangrenous festering and putrefaction. I died a thousand deaths when you sniffed your hair, because at that moment I saw the unpleasant realization in your expression that I was the source of the offending odor."

"Rank and putrid, your scent left a vile taste in my mouth and its bitter fumes set my eyes on fire," Jezebella complained.

"I'm so ashamed. I can't help the smell. It's from being dead nearly eighty-seven years."

"It took everything I had not to jump up and run from the room, but I caught myself and fought back that idea, thinking of my parents and the shame it would bring if I were expelled for rudeness on the first day at my new school. I don't know how, but I forced myself to stay in my seat," Jezebella went on.

"I wished a thousand times for a redo of that first day. The potency of your tomato juice scent took me completely by surprise. By the time I got home, I was a mental case and desperately needed to put some distance between us. By the next morning I was in Talkeetna."

96

"Edwin, Talkeetna is nearly 2400 miles from Full Moon. There is no way you drove there by the next morning."

"I know. But I simply took the same liberty that Stephenie took in *Twilight*, where she had Edward arriving in Alaska by the next morning."

"No way. That is clearly impossible. Edward's drive would have had to average more than 160 miles per hour."

"Yes, I know. By the next morning Edward would only have been somewhere in British Columbia. Even driving one-hundred miles per hour nonstop would have taken twenty-four hours and Edward would not have arrived in the Denali area until the next evening. It simply could not have happened the way it was written," I said.

"I guess we'll have to blame that goof on a failure to Google," Jezebella said. "So, what did you do in Alaska?"

"I spent two fantastic days with Anya.... I mean with my Talkeetna friends. It was great to see her.... them.... again. I recovered from my initial shock over you and realized that even as I craved your blood I was mesmerized, captivated, and spell-bound by you. I knew that I had to have you, even though we're dangerous for each other and any relationship between us may well end in something like a Shakespearean tragedy."

"I'm glad you came back. Knowing that you hunger for my blood makes wanting to be with you even more irrational, reckless, and crazy, but I crave that spine-chilling sensation of menace and fear that I feel in your presence. Being with you makes me feel like I'm Juliet sneaking Romeo into my bedroom with my parents at home, or maybe Eve stealing an apple from the Garden of Eden. Either way, Edwin, you are forbidden fruit, and tempting fate with you drives me wild with sweet terror."

"As I recall, things did not work out very well for either Juliet or Eve," I said.

"I must really be an idiot," Jezebella groaned.

"And yet, Romeo fell in love with the idiotic Juliet."

"What a glutton for punishment you must be," Jezebella said.

The sky was darkening with rain clouds and I began packing up our things to start on our way back home.

"We should get going now. I'd like to get back to the car before the rain starts," I said to Jezebella.

"I'll race you," Jezebella challenged as she took off running down the trail. "Watch how *I* travel through the forest!" she called back to me.

"Wait for me!" I called out as I ran after her. "I'm carrying this heavy backpack."

Jezebella flew through the forest, weaving effortlessly through the undergrowth and around trees as she maintained a lead of several yards, squealing and laughing as she ran. Then, suddenly, it was all over. I was running as fast as I could, trying to catch up with Jezebella before something happened to her, when I crashed into a tree and collapsed in a heap. I laid there among the ferns in a stupor for several minutes and then heard Jezebella talking to me.

"What happened, Edwin?" she asked, looking down at me.

"I think I might need some help," I said weakly.

"Are you hurt?" Jezebella asked.

"I don't know what happened. I was racing past the trees at deadly speed, like a bullet, missing them by mere inches. I must have miscalculated a turn."

"Exciting, isn't it?" Jezebella teased, grinning as she offered her hand to help me up.

"I may need to lie here for a bit," I wheezed.

"You're very pale looking, Edwin. More so than usual. Are you sure you're okay?"

"I'm fine," I responded. "I guess running through the forest probably wasn't the best idea, though."

"Let me carry the backpack for you," Jezebella offered.

"Show-off," I grumbled.

Arriving back at the car, we were reunited with Jezebella's protective entourage, which formed into a line behind the Yugo as we proceeded out of the forest. I was sure that Jezebella must have been thinking pleasant thoughts of our mostly perfect day. It had been a wonderful afternoon. Once we reached the main highway, we made good time back to Full Moon. I was anxious to get Jezebella home before Gnarly showed up and I pushed the Yugo to its limit. It was raining when we reached the Penguin house, but I remained dry because I had Jezebella hold an umbrella over me as I walked her to the front door.

"Jezebella, would you like to meet my family tomorrow? They are quite curious about you."

"Okay. I'm really curious about them too," Jezebella answered as she opened the door.

"Good. I'll see you in the morning."

Chapter 11.

MEETING THE DULLENS

I arrived at the Penguin home at ten Sunday morning. The temperature was a pleasant fifty-five degrees, and although it wasn't raining, the sky was dark with gray clouds and it was looking to be a very nice day. Jezebella was already up and dressed, waiting impatiently for my arrival.

"Edwin! Where have you been? I've been up since nine and waiting for hours!"

"Good morning. I see that you're fully dressed today," I snickered, noting that Jezebella was wearing a turtleneck sweater that completely covered her neck and throat, and that she wore a silver cross on a chain around her neck.

"I've had plenty of time to dress while waiting for you," she said sarcastically.

"Would you like to ride in the silver turtle again?" I asked. "I passed through the car wash on my way here."

"You probably shouldn't have done that," Jezebella replied. "You could have washed away the gunk that holds that sad vagabond of a car together."

"Careful. The silver turtle has feelings and is very sensitive."

"Face it, Edwin, your Yugo's only feelings are that it secretly wishes it had been born a Volvo."

"Why are you staring at me like that," I asked.

"Your eyes were amber, but today they're blue."

"Are you ready to go?" I asked in exasperation. "My family is very anxious to meet you."

"You know, Edwin, I don't even know where you live."

"You'll see soon enough," I responded.

We drove through town down Full Moon Avenue, past the library and the Bates Bed & Breakfast, past the Chinese restaurant and the bakery, past the sweet shop and that *Twilight* store where everybody gets dazzled, and then out of town on Highway 101 North. We continued to the Full Moon Wolf Refuge Center and then turned onto Pet Cemetery Drive, which winds through some very spooky hills. Driving through those hills always gives me the feeling that I'm being watched. It's creepy. We continued to the old Elizabeth Bathory house, where Pet Cemetery Drive turns southward and becomes Perdition Road.

"Edwin, is it much farther?"

"It's only a short distance more. We'll turn onto Elm Street at the end of the block, just past that last house on the left."

"You certainly do live in an interesting neighborhood," Jezebella remarked.

We turned onto Elm Street and just past the Krueger Estate we turned into a narrow driveway bordered on both sides by a high stone wall covered with green moss and overgrown with twisted, gnarly vines. Several yards down the driveway we came to an ancient, heavy iron gate that sags open in mock invitation with a "No Trespassing" sign hanging on the gatepost. A mailbox beside the gate bears the name Dullen, hand-printed in red letters. We entered the gate and drove a quarter-mile along a narrow road bordered on both sides by neatly cultivated rows of poison oak and hemlock, eventually coming to my house.

"Welcome to the Dullen house," I said.

"Wow! *This* is your house?" Jezebella stared at the house openmouthed and with eyes wide open in amazement.

The Dullen house has two floors. The lower floor is an old plantation style mansion right out of antebellum New Orleans, complete with the ghost of a vampire who was staked through the heart and decapitated as he slept one night. Argyle had the historic old house disassembled board by board and rebuilt here, minus the second floor. I'd like to say that the house was timeless and graceful, but its 155 years have left it decidedly timeworn and distressed, but not without a certain elegance. In glaring contrast, the custom-built upper floor is modern, trendy and sophisticated, with wide expanses of contemporary teak-framed glass offering breathtaking views of the surrounding woods and the nearby Sol Duc River. We chose the mismatched architecture for our home in tribute to the fickleness between the book and the movie.

"Impressive, isn't it. We cut down six huge, ancient cedars to make room for it."

"Edwin, there are six faces looking out that window at me."

"I told you they were anxious to meet you."

"Edwin, they're holding dinner forks!"

"Relax. They're just finishing Sunday brunch."

Getting out of the car, I walked around and opened Jezebella's door, pried her fingers loose from their death grip on the seatbelt, and dragged her out of the car. We then walked slowly up the pathway to the front porch.

"What are these plants along the walk and the front of the house, Edwin? All we had in Phoenix was cactus."

Joseph Veillon

"Rachel chose the mix. It's an assortment of foxglove, nightshade, hemlock, bleeding hearts, and narcissus. That's poison ivy along the driveway."

"What is that by the front door?"

"That's wolfsbane."

"Wow! Edwin. What is this huge plaque on the door?"

"This is the Dullen family crest. The oak shield was hand-carved by Irish monks in the fifth century. The gold forming the image was conjured by medieval French alchemists and the silver comes from melted coins looted by Scandinavian Vikings."

"What is that image?"

"It's Vlad Dracul," I answered, crossing myself thirteen times. "He personally sat for the sculptor over six hundred years ago."

Jezebella was no less spellbound with the interior of the unusual house as she was fascinated with its exterior. Having seen the oddness of the outside, she surely must have guessed that the interior would be very peculiar. The entry foyer contained several vintage glass-fronted cabinets displaying Argyle's collection of antique medical and bloodletting instruments, which would be the envy of any museum in the world. There were also priceless suits of armor and an amazing display of medieval weaponry and torture instruments used during the Inquisition.

"Wow! Edwin, this is fantastic. I'm amazed at what a cool house you have."

"Thanks. But you haven't seen anything yet," I said, leading Jezebella down a hall to a bank vault style steel security door. I punched in the ninety-eight digit security code and opened the door. Inside the room, the walls were lined with display cases containing Emrick's impressive collection of thousands of mounted and preserved butterflies. It was the most colorful and secure room in the house.

"Wow!" Jezebella exclaimed, dumbstruck with amazement. "This is fantastic. Words can't describe how beautiful, exquisite, magnificent, wonderful, incredible, mind-blowing, and unbelievable this is. I'm rendered completely speechless."

"It is quite beautiful. Emrick is extremely proud of his collection," I said, locking the door and leading Jezebella to the back of the house.

"Wow! Edwin. This is so awesome," she said, seeing that the entire rear wall of the house was made of glass. "But what happened to the glass? It's all cracked and pitted, like when a rock hits the windshield of a car."

"We installed the glass to have a good view of the swamp between our yard and the river. But the werewolves like to hit golf balls at the glass from the other side of the river."

Just at that moment, the mournful howls of several wolves rose from within the woods across the river. "Children of the night, go away!" I yelled at them.

"Edwin, what is that fence over there at the edge of the woods?"

"That's our deer pen," I replied.

I led Jezebella to the kitchen where the family was gathered around a computer screen, laughing hysterically at a Hillywood Show *Twilight* spoof on YouTube.

"Everyone, this is Jezebella Penguin," I announced.

"Hello Jezebella," the family said together in perfect unison.

"Jezebella, you've already met Argyle," I said.

"Yes, I have. Argyle treated the two concussions, sprained ankle, broken middle finger and numerous bruises that you've given me, not to mention my assorted self-inflicted injuries. It's nice to see you again Argyle," Jezebella said, waving her broken middle finger at me.

"I'm happy to see you under nonemergency conditions," Argyle said.

"Jezebella, this is Carmilla," I said.

"Hello Carmilla," Jezebella responded. "You have a very bizarre house."

"Thank you dear. Our home is your home," Carmilla answered.

"Carmilla, you're so beautiful. You look like you could be the star of an old horror movie," Jezebella said.

"Thank you, Jezebella. You're so flattering."

"Argyle likes to brag that he turned Carmilla twice, once when he made her a vampire, and again when he married her," I said.

"Argyle has a mystical way with women," Carmilla added, giving him a knowing wink.

"Hello, Jezebella. I'm Rachel. Please excuse my manners, but I want to finish my salad."

"Okay. See you later then," Jezebella answered.

"And this is Emrick," I added.

"Hello, Emrick. I really love your butterfly collection. It's awesome."

"Thank you," Emrick answered in his quiet, soft voice.

Just then, there was a commotion of dancing happy little feet and two more members of our family ran into the kitchen and romped playfully all around Jezebella's ankles.

"They're so adorable!" Jezebella exclaimed, bending down to pat our two pet dachshunds.

"Meet Nosferatu and Barnabas," I said.

"Oh, wow! They are so cute."

At that moment Allison and Neville appeared, sliding down the brass pole from the upper floor. The pole was from an old firehouse and was rarely used for anything other than Rachel's dancing.

"Hello, Jezebella," Allison said with a huge smile as she hugged Jezebella.

"Hello, Allison," Jezebella said. "I hope that we can be friends."

"I'm sure that we will, but then, the future is very subjective," Allison responded. "Edwin was right – you do smell like tomato juice."

"Hello, Jezebella. I'm Neville."

"Pleased to meet you, Neville," Jezebella replied. "You're all so perfect."

"Thank you. We really are quite perfect and beautiful," the entire family replied as one.

"We shouldn't boast. It's rude," Carmilla blushingly scolded everyone.

"Edwin, show Jezebella the rest of the house," Allison suggested.

I took Jezebella to the large family room at the west end of the house. The room was completely empty, except for a magnificently ornate jukebox sitting on a raised platform at one end of the room with hundreds of vinyl records neatly stacked on the floor all around it.

"Isn't it beautiful?" Carmilla said, more as a statement than a question. "Edwin found it at a flea market in Vancouver. It was a mess, but he restored it perfectly."

"It really is beautiful, and I've never seen so many records," Jezebella answered.

"Edwin is very musical. He's been collecting records for quite a few years now," Carmilla added. "Edwin, play something for Jezebella."

I took a quarter from the jar atop the jukebox and dropped it into the coin slot as the family gathered around.

"You inspired me to get this one," I said to Jezebella as "Dracula's Wedding" by OutKast began booming from the jukebox.

"That's so cool," Jezebella said. "I can't believe you got that song because of me."

"It's about a vampire who waits his whole life to find the right one to bite, but then he freaks out when he finally finds her. I can relate," I said.

"Will you play "Bloodletting" for me?" Jezebella asked.

I put another quarter into the jukebox and selected the requested song. Everyone joined in and sang "Bloodletting" for Jezebella, grooving and swaying to the beat of the jukebox. It's one of our favorite vampire songs.

"Disco! Disco! Play some disco Edwin!" The whole family loves disco and soon the house rocked as we boogied to "Dancing Queen," "Hot Stuff," "Le Freak," "YMCA," and "Stayin' Alive." Emrick and Rachel are especially accomplished disco dancers, and I taught Jezebella how to do "The Hustle." Unable to control her penchant for dirty dancing, Jezebella's moves soon morphed into some rather rude gyrations and the family slowly drifted away in embarrassed silence. Sometimes they could be such puritans. In fact, though, Argyle actually hung out with the Puritans back in the day.

"Would you like to see upstairs?" I asked Jezebella.

"Sure. You bet I do."

Taking Jezebella by the hand, I led her up the stairs toward the second floor.

"What is all of this on the wall, Edwin?"

"These are my diplomas. I've earned fifteen high school diplomas and several university degrees in various subjects."

"This is so impressive, Edwin. I'm going to need summer school just to graduate from Full Moon High School."

"One of my degrees is in English and I'm thinking about writing a novel."

"You know, having a degree in English doesn't make you a writer."

"I see your point," I reluctantly admitted.

"Maybe someday Stephen King will teach a writing class that you could take."

"You know, I really don't know how I managed to get all of these degrees. I must have had a lot of social promotions."

"What do you mean?"

"According to Stephenie in her official Twilight Saga guide, all mental and emotional development stops at the age at which a person is transformed into a vampire. I was only seventeen when I became a vampire. I don't know how I could possibly have acquired all of this knowledge or developed my sophisticated adult maturity. I must truly have been a teenage genius."

"Okay, Einstein, I'm duly impressed. Can I see the rest of the house now?"

"Of course you can. Follow me."

Chapter 12.

TWICE BITTEN

Continuing up the stairs, I led Jezebella into the second floor hallway, a long, spacious corridor with heavy wooden doors along both sides. At each end of the hall is a large window with a panoramic view of the grounds below. The various doors lead into our personal rooms, Argyle's office, a game room, a very interesting library, and a room known simply as "the vault." A small stand at the top of the stairs holds a statue of Nyx, the Greek goddess of the night.

"The upper level is quite different from downstairs. As you can see, the design is very modern and futuristic. We each have our own room with excellent views of the surrounding woods. This is my room," I said, stopping outside the door bearing my name engraved on a brass plaque and putting my key into the heavy old lock.

I opened the door and stood aside for Jezebella to enter. Watching her closely, I could see the look of amazement on her face as she scanned the room, appreciating my extensive collections of *Looney Tunes* posters, Smurfs, and *Peanuts* collectibles.

"More music?" she asked, noting the numerous CDs on my desk.

"Music is my passion. I'm crazy about disco and music from the eighties."

I turned on the stereo and "Talking in Your Sleep" by The Romantics began playing—*"I hear the secrets that you keep, when you're talking in your sleep."*

"Edwin, will you tell me about your past?"

"I was born Edwin Xavier Van Helsing in New Orleans, Louisiana. Perhaps fatefully, my birth occurred at Saint Jude Hospital, named for the patron saint of lost souls. My chronological age is 103 years, 8 months, and 21 days, but physically I appear to be 17 years old, the age at which my human life ended and when I was reborn to my vampire life. I have been a vampire for 86 years, 5 months, and 26 days.

My parents were Edwin and Elizabeth Van Helsing. Their parents were Dutch-German immigrants to New Orleans. Mom and dad met at a Mardi Gras masquerade ball while attending Bram Stoker College in New Orleans. My mother graduated with a degree in Gothic literature and took a job teaching at the Vixen-Hellcat School for Girls. My father attended Bram Stoker College for two years and then transferred to the Shyster School of Law. He graduated in 1900 and went to work for the old and distinguished New Orleans law firm of Lioncourt and Ponte du Lac.

My father was an honest man and didn't make much money as a lawyer, but my grandfather had made a fortune running a gambling house and by smuggling untaxed liquor and cigarettes from Cuba through the swamps around New Orleans, and he left my father a sizable inheritance. Those contraband earnings allowed my father to provide a very comfortable living for my mother, sister, and me. We lived in a creepy old haunted mansion at the corner of Bourbon and Whitechapel in the French Quarter, right across the street from Shady Sadie's Dance Hall and Madame de Pompadour's Bordello. My childhood was indeed a very happy time. My sister, Anna, and I liked hanging out at Marie Laveau's Voodoo Parlor and playing hide-and-seek among the tombs of Saint Louis Cemetery. Anna was three years younger than me. She had coal black hair, brown eyes, and olive skin. She looked just like our Italian maid.

The Infamous Zombie-Werewolf-Vampire Plague of 1918 struck New Orleans during the second week of September. It was the year that I graduated high school for the first time. At first, the creatures drifted into town only a few at a time, but within a week the city was swarming with dozens of bad-tempered, ill-humored, unsightly, and foul-smelling zombies, werewolves, and vampires who bit and slobbered on any human they could catch.

Most of our neighborhood was decimated, but we hung crosses, garlic, and wreaths of wolfsbane all around the outside of our house and the contemptible fiends left us alone, except that our dog disappeared. One night, though, I snuck out of the house to visit my girlfriend, Mary Jane Kelly, who worked at Madame de Pompadour's. I was attempting to sneak into the bordello from the back alley off Whitechapel Street, and—*sacré bleu!*—I was attacked by a *loup garou*—an odious, cursed, detestable French werewolf. The filthy, despicable *chien bâtard* bit me on the buttocks. The vile beast then put its hideous snout right in my face and growled menacingly, and it's sickening, rancid breath immediately turned my stomach and caused me to puke all over myself. *Quelle dommage!* I collapsed and lay in the gutter, crying in my wretched misery and hopelessness. My fate was sealed. I was doomed, ruined, condemned. Within a few hours, I would turn into a vile, disgusting French werewolf. *Quelle horreur! Zut alors!*

I remember Argyle kneeling over me and muttering quietly to himself as he examined me. He grabbed me by the collar and dragged me along the bumpy plague-ridden streets to his mansion near the swamp at the edge of town. If given in time, a vampire bite can reverse the werewolf infection, but at the price of the victim becoming a vampire instead. You might think that transforming me into a vampire may have presented Argyle with some kind of moral dilemma, but such was not the case. Allowing me to become such a damnable *bête noire* as a werewolf was unthinkable. No self-respecting vampire would ever permit such a ruinous lupine catastrophe to befall any human.

Argyle acted as soon as he got me home, for I was very nearly out of time. The staggering, razor-sharp coldness of his bite jarred me from the delirium of my hellish wolf-induced fever. I felt as if I were one of those crazy Norwegians jumping from a steam sauna into the frigid waters of the Arctic Ocean. The excruciating pain of the icy shock was like a full-body brain freeze. I felt as if I was being frozen alive, literally turning into a Popsicle. The pain was as if I had suffered a paper cut, been hit by a soft breeze, punched by a baby, trampled by a Chihuahua, and submerged in an herbal mud bath all at the same time.

Argyle almost found me too late. As his vampire antibodies battled the werewolf contagion for control of my body, werewolf hair appeared on my palms and I kept lifting my leg whenever I needed to pee. I even howled at the moon several times during the course of the night. Throughout the seemingly endless night, I lay in Argyle's bed writhing in frigid pain, my body torn between the vampire and the werewolf. By sunrise the next morning Argyle's bite had succeeded in causing my body to reject the werewolf virus and I had become a vampire. I woke up in a state of confused lethargy, not yet fully comprehending what had happened to me. Argyle would soon explain the details.

At first, I was angry and resentful that Argyle had changed me into a leechlike, parasitical, bloodsucking monster. Vampires were merciless creatures who preyed on the innocent and doomed their victims to eternal damnation, forever hungry, famished, and ravenous for human blood. Imagine my revulsion when I learned that Argyle had changed me into one of these corpselike, ghoulish, cadaverous, undead fiends. During those confusing first days, even after Argyle told me his story, I was unable to see myself as anything but a repulsive abomination, doomed for all eternity to a wicked, nefarious life in the dank, gloomy shadows of the world. I was down in the dumps, melancholic, depressed, and thoroughly bummed out.

However, Argyle convinced me that I could live among humans as he did. In addition, when I noticed what a stylish, fashionable and trendy dresser Argyle was and that he lived in a fine house, I decided that the vampire life might not be so bad after all. The deal was sealed when Argyle stood me in front of a mirror and I saw how totally perfect and beautiful I had become. I looked positively dazzling. I moved in with Argyle and became his eager student. Argyle taught me about vampires, werewolves, fashion, etiquette, and grooming, and I learned to live with style, elegance, and class. Such was the beginning of my undead life.

Argyle was exceptionally narcissistic and living with him eventually became unendurable. To make matters worse, after Argyle married Carmilla, having newlyweds in the house all the time became a nuisance. It was also quite embarrassing, after all, Carmilla was supposed to be my sister. And, despite the glamour of vampire life, I never truly felt comfortable with my vampire existence. It was as if I was in the wrong skin. I could never quite put my finger on it, but something deep in my soul seemed to be at odds with what I had become, as if I was meant to be something else. After a few years, I ran away, joined the Cirque des Lunatiques, and went out into the world on my own.

I traveled with the lunatics for several years, secretly taking blood from the circus animals in the dark of night. I felt

Joseph Veillon

guilty about taking blood from weak and frail caged animals. It wasn't sporting and I could see in their eyes how sad and wounded they felt. Eventually, my illicit nocturnal feasting came to weigh profoundly on my conscience, and the moral impoverishment caused by taking advantage of defenseless and vulnerable captive animals became more than I could bear. One night, I set all of the animals free and left the lunatics. I returned to Argyle and Carmilla and vowed that I would feed only on human blood from that time on."

"That is so cool, Edwin. You're an animal lover. That story I heard about you must be true."

"What story are you talking about?"

"Elliot told me that you snuck into school one night and freed all the frogs in the biology lab."

"Yes. I'm guilty as charged. There were frogs hopping around Full Moon High School for weeks. Principal Forks was not amused."

Just as I was about to grab Jezebella and throw her into an iron cage bound with iron chains, Rachel and Neville walked into my room, their interruption bringing me back to my senses. Reliving my circus days must have given me a flashback.

"The ice will be good tonight," Rachel announced.

"Tonight might be our last chance," Neville added. "The weather will be warming up and the ice will soon be too soft."

"We've already asked the others. Everyone is getting ready," Rachel said.

"I'm in," I stated. "Neville is right. The ice won't last much longer."

"We're meeting in an hour," Rachel said.

"Would you like to come with us?" I asked Jezebella.

"What are you talking about and where are we going?" she asked.

"We're going ice skating," I told her.

"Ice skating? Where can you go ice skating anywhere around Full Moon?"

"There's a pond not far from here that freezes over in winter. No one else knows about it," I explained.

"But it doesn't get cold enough here for a pond to freeze that hard," Jezebella protested.

"Just go with it, Jezebella. It's fantasy," Rachel said.

"Okay. That sounds cool. I'll go."

Chapter 13.

THE GAME

Gnarly's green game warden Land Rover was parked in front of the Penguin house when I brought Jezebella home to change her clothes. Finding Gnarly at home was a fortuitous co-incidence. I would finally be able to meet Jezebella's father. I parked in the street behind Gnarly's vehicle, helped Jezebella out of the car, and walked with her to the front door of the house.

"Is that you sweetheart?" Gnarly called from somewhere within the house.

"Hi dad," Jezebella called out as we walked through the house toward Gnarly's voice.

We found Gnarly sitting at the dining room table cleaning his weapons. Laid out on the table before him were two .45 caliber Glock pistols, an Israeli Uzi submachine gun, a 12-gauge double-barreled shotgun, a sniper rifle, a tranquilizer rifle, and a Taser. A half-eaten pizza and several cans of Witches Brew, a boutique beer brewed right here in Full Moon with water recycled from the sewage plant, also occupied the table.

"Hi dad," Jezebella repeated as we entered the dining room.

"Hello sweetheart," Gnarly said, looking up. "I see you brought a friend."

"Dad, this is Edwin."

"Hello, Edward."

"Dad, his name is Edwin."

"Hello, Chief Penguin. I want to formally, officially, properly, and legally introduce myself. I'm Edwin Dullen."

"Nice to meet you, Edward. Call me Gnarly. What are you crazy kids up to?"

"It's *Edwin,* dad! His name is *Edwin!*"

"I've invited Jezebella to go ice skating with my family," I said.

"Ice skating in Full Moon?" Gnarly said suspiciously.

"Just go with it, dad. It's fantasy." Jezebella then bounded up the stairs. "I need to change clothes. I'll be right back."

"Have a seat, Edward. Check out my new gutting knife. Feel the balance and razor-sharp edge of the lethal blade. This knife is so sharp that it could easily cut right through stone," Gnarly said as he affectionately caressed the largest and most dangerous looking knife I had ever seen. "I expect you to take very good care of my baby girl. Jezebella is all I live for, if you understand my meaning."

"Don't worry, Chief Penguin," I stuttered. "I promise to bring Jezebella back to you unharmed, undamaged, unscratched, unblemished, unsullied, and unchanged."

"You know, *Edwin,* I'm down with the kids and I know what you'll be thinking when you look at my little girl. Just remember, Jezebella is my only daughter and I will know if *anything* happens."

"I promise, Chief Penguin, I'll think of Jezebella as if she were mind-numbingly plain and ordinary," I said, wondering what Gnarly would do if he knew about our naughty skinny-dipping yesterday.

"Good boy. Call me Gnarly. Hand me a fresh cold one."

"I hope you boys are getting along," Jezebella said as she came down the stairs.

"Gnarly and I were just bonding," I said, rising from my chair.

"You crazy kids have fun," Gnarly said as he stuffed a can of triple strength grizzly bear pepper spray into Jezebella's bag.

"Dad, this isn't necessary. Don't worry about me. I'll be fine."

"Jezebella is in good hands," I said.

"You watch those hands and have my baby girl home early," Gnarly commanded, putting down his cleaning cloth and dramatically snapping closed his shotgun.

"*Dad!*" Jezebella groaned.

"Just keeping it real," Gnarly replied.

Wasting no time getting out of the house, I quickly got Jezebella into the car and started the engine. It gasped and wheezed to life and we were soon on a winding road that meandered aimlessly through the forest east of Full Moon. We drove until the pavement ended, where we were forced to leave the car and hike to the pond, leaving a trail of Reese's Pieces to guide us back to the car. We trudged through the forest, hacking our way through a jungle of thick vegetation and even fighting off a pair of psychotic squirrels and a swarm of killer bees along the way. After narrowly escaping capture by a family of hunting Sasquatch, we fought off a horde of malarial mosquitos, barely avoided a bottomless quicksand pit, and navigated a treacherous crossing of a slow moving, ankle deep stream. When we eventually arrived at the pond my family was already there waiting for us, their cars parked in the neat clearing beside the pond. They must have taken the road from the other side of the forest.

"*Holy haunted forest!* You really do have a frozen ice skating pond," Jezebella said.

"These are for you," I said, producing a pair of new ice skates.

"You know how uncoordinated and physically incompetent I am. I nearly drowned crossing that ankle deep stream. I can't skate."

"Relax, Jezebella. Just mimic what everyone else is doing."

At that very moment, Rachel and Emrick glided past, skating together with flawless grace and elegance, then executing impeccable triple Lutz jumps in perfect unison before skating off across the ice. Argyle and Carmilla sashayed past, twirling in perfectly synchronized side-by-side shotgun spins and looking as if they should be on tour with Stars on Ice.

"I could never do anything like that," Jezebella said with appreciative envy and jealousy. "Can we play baseball instead?"

"You'll do fine. I'll lead you around until you get used to the skates," I said as I tied her laces.

"I hope you have a few years to spare," she remarked sarcastically.

"Time means nothing to me," I said, checking my watch, a ten-year calendar, and the position of the sun.

Allison and Neville then skimmed by, holding hands and looking like true skating professionals, each of them launching into a triple toe loop worthy of Olympic gold, landing effortlessly and finishing with perfectly matched layback spins. As I led Jezebella onto the ice, we suddenly heard the music of imaginary Spanish guitars and saw Argyle and Carmilla across the pond ice dancing an impassioned flamenco. Not to be outdone, Emrick and Rachel commenced a sizzling Argentine tango, while Neville and Allison launched into a sultry Latin rumba. Their scorching dance moves threatened to melt the ice on which we stood and dump us into the murky depths of the knee-deep pond.

Then, in an instant, it all came undone. While attempting to execute an elaborate and complicated beginner's twirl Jezebella slipped from my grasp and went spinning wildly out of control across the ice. She smashed first into Allison and Neville, knocking them off their feet, and seconds later crashed into Rachel and Emrick, rebounding off Emrick but dragging Rachel down with her. Trying to stop her head-over-heels tumble to certain calamity Jezebella reached out as she flew past and grabbed Carmilla by the leg, causing Carmilla and Argyle to career off the ice and into a snow bank at the edge of the pond.

Having caused more mayhem, havoc, chaos, bedlam, and pandemonium than a vampire crashing a werewolf convention, Jezebella finally spun to a stop and lay on her back staring upward in dazed bewilderment. It was a catastrophe not unlike the carnage that would be left in the aftermath of a blind man's demolition derby.

Then we saw them—four vampires standing in the woods at the edge of the pond, only a few feet from where Jezebella lay on the ice recovering her senses. We instantly rushed to Jezebella and gathered possessively around her. The visitors, a male and three females who all appeared to be about nineteen or twenty years old, stepped warily from the woods, eyeing us as if they had never seen ice skating vampires.

All four vampire strangers wore long hair with colorful cloth headbands, leather sandals, bell-bottomed jeans, brightly colored tie-dyed shirts, and an assortment of love beads, braided hemp bracelets, and peace sign medallions. A couple of them also wore fringed suede leather vests. These vampires were clearly hippie flower children from the 1960s scene. The male hippie vampire was casually tossing a baseball back and forth from one hand to the other.

Joseph Veillon

"Peace, love, and welcome friends. My name is Argyle and these beautiful vampires are my family."

"Man, that's like, groovy. My name is Lamont," said the male vampire, who wore granny glasses and looked just like John Lennon. "This is Moonbeam," he added, introducing a petite Asian female who also wore granny glasses and had long, black hair.

"Peace and love," Moonbeam said, flashing us the peace sign with both hands. "Your ice dancing is really far out."

"Thank you. We really dig your cool hippie threads," Allison and Rachel responded together.

"I'm Venus," said the second female, a slender ebony beauty with luscious dark caramel colored skin and a huge afro-style hairdo. "Your skating is like, happening. You vamps are really down with it."

"Thanks. You're pretty hip looking yourselves," said Emrick.

"This is so cool. My name is Andromeda," said the third female, a pretty blonde with white daisies in her hair.

"What brings you hippies to our neighborhood?" Argyle asked.

"We're traveling from San Francisco on our way to Quebec for a love-in, and after that we're going to England for the Summer Solstice Festival at Stonehenge," Lamont explained.

"Edwin, I didn't think that black vampires existed," Jezebella whispered. "According to Stephenie in her official Twilight Saga guide, all vampires are supposed to be extremely pale regardless of their original ethnicity."

"That is what she wrote, but black vampires are well documented in cinema. *Blacula*, *Vampire in Brooklyn*, *Queen of*

124

the Damned, Vamp, Dracula 2000, and *Blade* are all movies with black vampires."

"Don't forget about Laurent in that *Twilight* movie," Jezebella added. "He was a cool dude."

"Yes. Laurent was very obviously black in the movie. I don't know why Stephenie would write such a blatant contradiction of established cinematic fact."

"The girl is human?" the hippie vampires all asked at once, their eyes wide with astonishment and incredulity as they each turned their full attention to Jezebella.

"Yes. She is with us," Argyle said.

"You have a pet human?" Lamont asked.

"She must be a good luck charm," Andromeda guessed.

"Or maybe she's a witch," Moonbeam speculated.

"Jezebella is with me," I said. "She is not a pet, charm, or witch."

"She must be very special for you to resist her scent and allow her to be with you," Venus observed.

"She is just an ordinary, plain, and unremarkable girl," I stated.

"We'd like to have such a human," Lamont said. "Would you sell her?"

"I'm sorry, but Jezebella is not for sale," Argyle answered.

"Could we trade something for her?" asked Moonbeam.

"She is with me and is not available," I stated firmly.

"But we really want her. Surely we can work something out," Andromeda offered.

"We simply must have her," Lamont declared, and the hippie vampires quickly gathered around him and staged a sit-in, spreading blankets on the ground and singing "All You Need is Love" by The Beatles.

125

We immediately jumped between Jezebella and the hippie vampires and assumed tai chi poses. The "make love not war" flower child vampires would never get past us.

"Chill out brothers and sisters. I'm sure we can reach a peaceful agreement," Lamont implored.

"We would be very nice to her," Andromeda promised. "She would be our little sister."

"Yes. Our little sister," Moonbeam and Venus repeated.

"Perhaps we could share the girl," Lamont offered.

"Jezebella is with me," I said sternly. "She is not going anywhere."

"It seems that we have a quandary," Argyle observed.

"Yes. A real impasse," Emrick added with a wide grin while stretching his arms out before him and cracking his knuckles.

"Stop it!" Jezebella exclaimed. "I don't want anyone fighting over me. From now on, I'm Scotland."

"What?" my family and the hippies all asked together, everyone looking totally puzzled, bewildered, befuddled, and mystified.

"I think you meant to say Switzerland," I said.

"What do you mean?" Jezebella asked.

"Scotland is the home of that gastronomic treat known as haggis, the Loch Ness Monster, men wearing kilts, those crazy socks, the finest single malt whisky in the world, and Doonies Farm in Aberdeen," I said.

"What are you talking about?" Jezebella asked, her voice dripping with exasperation.

"You meant to say that you were Switzerland, to indicate your neutral status."

"Scotland—Switzerland—whatever. I will not be the cause of any fighting. You hippie vampires are cool, but I'm with Edwin."

"I'm afraid I must insist that we vampires decide the matter," Lamont declared. "Vampire bylaws demand a resolution between vampires. The human girl cannot make the decision."

"Lamont is correct," Argyle agreed. "The rules require that the dispute be settled between vampires."

"I suggest a contest. The winner gets the girl," Lamont offered.

"What do you have in mind?" Argyle asked.

"Do you play baseball?" Lamont asked.

"Baseball makes too much noise," Neville answered.

"We could arm wrestle," Emrick proposed.

"What about volleyball?" Moonbeam asked.

"How about a poker tournament?" Rachel offered.

"We could run a race," Venus said.

"What about a Scrabble tournament?" Carmilla suggested.

"A Scrabble tournament! That is a really hip idea. I dig it," Lamont said.

And so it happened that we invited the hippie vampires to our home and held a Scrabble tournament with Jezebella Penguin as the prize. The hippie vampires were totally relentless, vicious, and brutal in their gameplay. Never before had we encountered such coldblooded, hardnosed, and unsympathetic word warriors. These hippies were Scrabble samurai. Taking no chances with her safety, we locked Jezebella in a closet upstairs in Argyle's soundproof office with Nosferatu and Barnabas posted as guards for the duration of the tournament.

We played a marathon of 666 games of Scrabble in a 24-hour period. It was an exhausting, grueling, arduous effort, but

Allison played supercalifragilisticexpialidocious to win the last game, and we massacred the hippie vampires by one game. The hippies were terribly disappointed about losing and having to leave without Jezebella, but the hippies were good sports and bore their shame with grace. Jezebella was safe, although her eyes were a bit light sensitive from being in the dark closet for 24 hours. *Go Team Edwin!*

"You vamps are really hip," Lamont said.

"And you hippies are groovy," Argyle replied.

"You're all totally cool. Come back and visit anytime," Carmilla added.

"You're going to miss the love-in," Andromeda said sadly to Jezebella.

"I'll catch another one someday, maybe next year," Jezebella answered. "Peace out."

"Peace out," the hippie vampires all said together, each of them flashing us the peace sign.

The hippies piled into their psychedelic VW van and drove away. None of us had ever met hippie vampires before. It was a far out, mind-blowing experience.

"Jezebella, have you given any more thought to joining my family?" I asked when we were alone.

"No, Edwin, I haven't changed my mind about becoming a vampire."

"Jezebella, you don't know what you'd be giving up if you remain human. If you would join us, you would never need to worry about nomads or other vampires."

"I simply can't do it, Edwin. As long as I'm human, I will always be plain and monotonous, but at least that way you will stay interested in me. I know that it's my pallid personality that attracts you. If I were to become a vampire, you would soon lose

128

interest in me and then you would go looking for another ordinary, boring girl. It would be just like what happens when people get married."

"Don't say no right now, Jezebella. Give me six months to persuade you."

"No, Edwin."

"One year, then. Just one year," I implored.

"No way. You'll never convince me."

"Two years. At least give me two years, *please*."

"What part of *no* don't you understand?"

"Three years?" I begged.

"It's never going to happen, Edwin. Forget about it."

"Five years," I pleaded. *"Please!* Five is my limit."

"No, no, *no*, Edwin. I do not want to ever be a vampire."

"Jezebella, you really do not understand what you're missing. You know, once you've tried vampire, you'll never go back."

"Edwin, I just don't want to be a vampire. I can't handle the thought of it. I'm happy with my ordinary human life. Besides, I'm still a virgin."

"Whoa, wait…. what did you say?"

"Even if I wanted to become a vampire, I can't. I'm still a virgin," Jezebella said, the flirtatious tone in her voice subtle, but unmistakable.

"Jezebella, before you my life was as dark as a moonless night, but now, all of a sudden, things are looking much brighter, as if illuminated by the light of a full moon."

"Edwin, can't we just continue our frivolous relationship and not expect anything meaningful out of it? We have plenty of time."

Joseph Veillon

"It's okay, Jezebella. I understand, but I want you to know that I'm not giving up. I'll be keeping a close eye on you and waiting for you to change your mind."

Chapter 14.

THE DREAM

And so it was that Jezebella finally turned down my offer of timeless undead immortality and everlasting resplendence. Of course, I also had the trifling conspiratorial and underhanded motive of eluding the scrutiny of the Vultures, but my selfish intentions toward Jezebella were pure. My family was deeply disappointed and saddened that Jezebella had declined to join our vampire clan. Everyone worried that the Vultures would come and that I would be forced to marry Paine. I would have no choice. Refusal would result in vampire excommunication and revocation of my Club Vamp privileges. The shame on my family would be unspeakable.

Despite all of this, Jezebella's succulent tomato juice scent continued to tease my olfactory senses while her mind-numbing monotony unceasingly stirred my licentious yearnings. Even though Jezebella had refused to become a vampire, I had no desire to end our shallow relationship. Just as it happened in *Twilight,* our nonsensical mutual obsession bound us together like oil and water. Besides, an old crone Gypsy fortune teller with a traveling Romanian carnival mysteriously foretold that Jezebella would ultimately join me "in the fourth book." Although this vague prophecy gave me a measure of hope, I was grief-stricken at the thought of suffering through three more volumes of this sleepy literary impersonation.

Days went by. Weeks passed. No one knows what happened during the shadowy, unexplained period following Jezebella's close encounter with fate at the hands of those nomadic wanderers. Whatever transpired between the night of that notorious event and prom night went unrecorded and remains shrouded in mystery to this day.

Sitting in the kitchen of the Penguin home, I sipped from a glass of warm tomato juice and listened to "Love Song for a Vampire" by Annie Lennox while Jezebella dressed upstairs. Tonight is the highly anticipated occasion of the glamorous annual bash known as the Full Moon High School prom. The theme this year is *Saturday Night Fever.* The only social event in town more anticipated than the high school prom is the annual Halloween dance at the Full Moon Senior Center.

My silent musing was interrupted by a somewhat hesitant knock on the front door.

"Edwin, would you mind getting the door?" Jezebella called from upstairs.

Upon opening the door, I was greeted by the sight of Tyson Fryer, dressed in an ill-fitting, brown polyester leisure suit.

"Hello, Tyson. May I help you?"

"Is Jezebella at home?" he timidly inquired.

"Is she expecting you?" I asked.

"I've come to take her to prom," Tyson replied.

"I'm sorry, Tyson. There must be some mistake. Jezebella is going to the prom with me."

"She should have been expecting me. I've been telling everyone at school for weeks that we were going to prom together."

"You are quite the Casanova, Tyson, but I really am very sorry. Perhaps we'll see you at the dance," I said, closing the door.

"Who was that at the door?" Jezebella called from upstairs.

"It was Tyson Fryer. He was here to take you to the prom."

"That boy is totally delusional," she answered.

Just as I sat down again, there was another knock at the door. This time it was Elliot, who, like Tyson, was dressed in a brown leisure suit apparently purchased at the thrift store.

"Hello, Elliot. May I help you?"

"Is Jezebella at home?" he hesitantly inquired.

"Is she expecting you?" I asked.

"I've come to take her to prom," Elliot replied.

"I'm sorry, Elliot. There must be some misunderstanding. Jezebella is attending the prom with me. I really am very sorry. Perhaps we'll see you at the dance," I said.

"Who is that at the door?" Jezebella called from upstairs.

"It's Elliot. He wants to take you to the prom."

"You tell Elliot to get over to Angelica's house right away. I happen to know that she asked him to the prom and at this very minute she is home waiting for him to pick her up. And tell him to be sure that he tells Angelica that I was his first choice."

I had just settled back into my chair with a fresh warm tomato juice when there was another knock at the door. This time it was a very uneasy looking Fig, dressed in a brown leisure suit that also undoubtedly came from the thrift store.

"Hello, Fig. May I help you?"

"Is Jezebella at home?" he warily inquired.

"Have you come to ask her to the prom?"

"Why…. yes, I have," Fig replied. "How did you know?"

"I'm sorry, Fig, but you must have gotten the wrong impression about something. Jezebella is going to the prom with me."

"Who is it, Edwin?" Jezebella called from upstairs.

"It's Fig. He wants to take you to the prom."

"You tell Fig to get himself over to Jessica's house right now. At this very minute she is sitting at home waiting for him to ask her to the dance. And tell him to be sure that he tells Jessica that I was his first choice."

"You heard the lady, Fig. I really am very sorry. Perhaps we'll see you at the dance," I said, closing the door.

Just as I had settled back into my chair to finish my warm tomato juice there was yet another knock at the door. *This place is busier than the blood bar at a vampire convention!* This time it was Selene, in a very short, sexy black dress that bared her lovely, pale shoulders. Her beauty took my breath away.

"Hello, Selene. May I help you?"

"Hello, Edwin, is Jezebella at home?" she inquired. "I've come to ask if she would be my prom date."

"Who is that at the door?" Jezebella called from upstairs.

"It's Selene. She wants to be your prom date."

"Selene? Really? Is she wearing that sexy black dress?"

"Yes, she certainly is," I replied.

"Tell her to come on up," Jezebella responded.

As Selene ran upstairs I sat down and replayed "Love Song for a Vampire," wondering if I was about to be dumped and replaced with the beautiful ninja girl. Selene soon came back down the stairs, giving me a wicked smile and a wink as she let herself out.

"Jezebella, what did you say to Selene?" I called out.

"I promised Selene that I would save her a couple of dances."

A few seconds later, Jezebella emerged from her room and began descending the stairs in awkward and inelegant slow motion, not being accustomed to wearing heels. She almost made it all the way down, but on the last step she lost her balance and tumbled forward. I moved quickly to catch her fall, but we collided, bumping heads and plummeting to the floor in a snarled heap.

Once we had regained consciousness and cleared our heads, I could not help but notice and admire the stunning contrast between Jezebella's ghostly pale skin and the vivid color of her red dress. Tonight, Jezebella's ordinary and unexceptional look was nothing short of breathtaking.

"Are you okay?" I asked Jezebella.

"I may not be coordinated enough to walk down the stairs but I can boogie," Jezebella declared.

"We have to make it to the dance alive first," I replied. "Here, let me pin this corsage on you."

"It's so beautiful," she said as I pinned the corsage of red and white orchids and miniature red roses to her dress.

Jezebella suddenly burst out laughing, and then doubled up in a mad fit of laughing, giggling, and snickering. She was having such comical hysterics that I wondered if she had suffered another head injury in the fall.

"Why are you laughing?" I asked in confused amazement.

"I was just thinking about Bella in *Twilight*. How in the world could she not have known all along that she was going to prom that evening? Besides the posters that would have covered nearly every exposed surface at school, prom would have been the number one topic of conversation for days. I mean, come on, she was wearing a formal dress and Edward showed up in a tuxedo. What were they having—a stealth prom? No one could be so utterly clueless."

"You're absolutely correct. Even Edward thought it was ridiculous."

"You know, Edwin, you're very handsome in your custom-made leisure suit."

"And you are simply dazzling. Shall we go?" I asked, opening the front door for Jezebella and then following her outside.

"Wow! Is that Argyle's Edsel?"

"He loaned it to me for the night."

"This is so cool, Edwin. Can I drive?"

"Didn't I just say something about getting to the dance alive?" I said as I opened the passenger door and helped Jezebella into the car. Sliding into the driver's seat, I noticed that Jezebella was wearing only one shoe.

"Where is your other shoe?"

"What do you mean, Edwin?" she asked, looking confused.

"You've only got one shoe," I pointed out.

"Oh!" she exclaimed as she looked down at her feet. Jezebella opened the car door and retrieved the shoe that had apparently fallen off as she got into the car. "Okay, I'm ready now."

We drove through town to the Bed Bug Inn and parked in the lot beside the meeting room annex where prom was being held. Many couples had already arrived and the shockwave of booming music could be felt resonating outside the building. I helped Jezebella out of the car and we took a place in line, waiting for our turn to walk through the archway at the entrance to the dance and have our photograph taken with a life-size cardboard cutout of John Travolta in that famous *Saturday Night Fever* pose. It was cheesy and embarrassing but it was fun.

The dance was already underway when we entered and the atmosphere was at once electrifying and spellbinding. The large meeting room had been converted into a very authentic looking 1970s discothèque, complete with mirrored disco ball, rotating multi-colored strobe lights, walls covered with glittering foil and thousands of tiny twinkling lights, and even a raised dance floor lighted from beneath with dozens of randomly pulsating colored lights. There was even a fog machine spewing wispy white vapor across the dance floor. It looked just like the disco club in the movie.

Emrick, Rachel, Neville, Allison, and about three dozen others were on the dance floor reenacting the "Night Fever" line dance from the movie. Rachel was unreservedly stunning in an elegant black dress that reached to just below her knees, and Allison looked utterly fabulous in a mid-calf length satiny blue dress, both of which were totally exquisite late 1970s retro. Emrick and Neville were resplendent in their custom-made white leisure suits that matched mine exactly. We had each chosen a Qiana shirt that color coordinated with our date's dress. We looked fabulous, and the girls looked pretty good too. Jezebella and I waded into the crowd and joined the dance, taking places in the line next to Neville and Allison.

Jezebella proved that she could party, boogie, work it, and get down with the best of us. The girl could definitely dance. Throughout the night, Jezebella showed off her superb flair for dirty dancing, at one point even leading a conga line of writhing dancers hilariously trying to imitate her seductive gyrations. More than one unfortunate boy incurred the wrathful rebuke of his date for staring too long at Jezebella, and Jezebella herself received several angry looks from infuriated girls.

"Would you like something to drink?" I asked Jezebella after several dances.

"Sure. I could use a break," she replied.

We made our way through the throng of dancers to the refreshment bar where, much to our astonishment, we found Jody Silver Bullet serving drinks and cleaning tables.

"I see that you've crashed our party," I joked.

"Hey, Jody," Jezebella said shooting me a reproving look.

"Hi, Jezebella," Jody replied self-consciously.

"You look taller since I saw you at the beach. Did you have a growth spurt?" Jezebella asked.

"It's just this box I'm standing on to see the dance floor," Jody replied. "Would you care for a refreshment?"

"I'd like a root beer," Jezebella answered.

"Do you have any tomato juice?" I inquired.

"No," Jody answered rather curtly.

"Then I'll have a root beer please. Why do you look so embarrassed, Jody?"

"Be nice, Edwin," Jezebella hissed. "What are you doing here, Jody?"

"The school is paying twenty dollars to kids willing to work the dance and humiliate themselves in front of their friends."

"Why do you say it like that?" Jezebella asked.

"Face it, Jezebella. The only kids working the dance are the ones who couldn't get dates. I could use the money though. I've had to replace a lot of clothes lately."

"Here are the cokes you wanted, Jody." It was Tyson Fryer, who had just come from a back room carrying a case of sodas.

"Thanks. Just put them on the table," Jody said.

"Hello, Tyson. I see that you made it to the dance after all," I remarked with scarcely concealed ridicule.

"Behave, Edwin," Jezebella sharply retorted. "Thanks for the root beer, Jody."

"You're welcome. But listen, I have a message for you from the wolves," Jody said, lowering his voice.

"What is it?" Jezebella asked.

"This is really stupid. Please don't be mad at me," Jody begged, looking extremely uncomfortable.

"Tell me. Just say it," Jezebella urged.

"I'm so sorry, Jezebella. The wolves want me to warn you about skinny-dipping in the woods. They said to tell you 'we'll be watching.'"

"Oh. So, they saw that, did they? I'm so plain and ordinary. Sorry they had to see that," Jezebella replied, obviously embarrassed.

"They didn't mind all that much," Jody snickered as his eyes roamed over Jezebella, appreciating her form beneath the thin red dress. "Should I tell them to butt out?"

"No, but thanks anyway for the warning," Jezebella replied.

"Let's get out of here," I said to Jezebella, having had enough of this conversation.

Taking her by the hand, I led Jezebella through the room, passing several of her friends along the way. Most were on the dance floor, but we noticed Jessica and Fig in a dark corner all knotted up in a heavy make-out session—talk about going all the way into the twilight! Angelica and Elliot, Samantha and Salem, Selene and Miriam were all slow dancing on the darkened dance floor. Victoria looked at us and blew a kiss as we passed. Reaching the door, we walked out into the cool dark of the night and left the thumping disco behind us.

I took Jezebella into the park across the street from the Bed Bug Inn, ignoring the sign that said PARK CLOSED AFTER DARK. We followed a brick pathway a few yards into the park to a gazebo flanked by a stone grotto with a gurgling water fountain that emptied into a small pool. I pulled Jezebella close to me and we slow danced as I hummed a romantic tune by Iron & Wine. After dancing together for a few minutes, Jezebella and I sat in the gazebo holding hands and smooching as the full moon rose in the sky and cast its beam across the shadowy black ghosts of the clouds passing in the breeze. A wolf pup howled feebly from somewhere across the street.

"Did you see that?" Jezebella asked as she got up to investigate. "Something fell over there in that corner."

"What is it?" I asked.

"Oh, look, Edwin. It's a flightless bird. It is so adorable. Can you put it back in the nest?"

"He is a cute little guy," I agreed as I lifted the unharmed bird back to its nest in the rafters of the gazebo.

"I hope it'll be okay," she said.

"Jezebella, there's something I should tell you," I said as I took her hand and pulled her close to me again.

"What is it, Edwin?" she said, gazing intently into my eyes.

"I'm afraid that I have an ulterior motive for bringing you here tonight."

"You mean some reason other than prom?" she asked, never moving her gaze from my face.

"You've become the most important part of my life, at least to the degree that an undead guy can have a life, and I want you to be with me for all eternity. I don't ever want to be without you."

"I assume you're talking about me becoming a vampire and joining your family?" Jezebella asked.

"Yes," I answered. "I can't imagine my life without you. I'm too weak and selfish to leave you alone. My desires are more important to me than your wishes."

"So you're seriously willing to transform me into a vampire, knowing that this would be the twilight of my plain, ordinary human existence, even though my pathetic life has barely begun. Edwin, I have my entire wearisome human life ahead of me. You would have me give up all of that? Seriously, would you take that away from me?"

"Every twilight is followed by a breaking dawn," I astutely observed. "You would trade your human dullness for the beauty and charismatic personality of a vampire."

"So, you were hoping that tonight would be a special occasion?" Jezebella asked. "You're ready to transform me right now?"

"If you're ready," I replied, drawing Jezebella closer and lowering my lips to hers. She melted her body into mine, surrendering herself to me completely, and passionately returning my kiss.

Jezebella's breathing quickened and her body trembled ever so slightly, a rosy blush coloring her cheeks. "I don't really know why I've held out and refused you for so long," Jezebella quietly admitted.

"Are you sure, Jezebella?" I asked, gently pulling my lips from hers and staring longingly into her eyes. "You're ready, tonight, at this very moment?"

"I'm sure, Edwin," she whispered, turning her head to the side and exposing her luscious, quivering neck to me. "I'm ready."

Admiring the pallid beauty of Jezebella's creamy skin, I breathed deeply of her fragrance, savoring her delicious scent, and then lowered my mouth to her neck....

"Edwin! Edwin!" I heard a dreamy, faraway voice calling my name, as if through a muffled tunnel. Through a haze of drowsy befuddlement, I realized that the voice belonged to Jezebella.

"Edwin! Wake up!" Jezebella urged in a hushed, but insistent tone. "You fell asleep during the movie. Class is over."

The icy cold touch of her hand on mine shocked me back to consciousness. "I had the strangest dream," I said, rubbing my eyes and yawning. "It was totally weird."

"What kind of dream was it," Jezebella asked.

"I just told you, it was a weird dream."

"No, Edwin. I meant what was your dream about?"

"Oh. It was so surreal. I dreamed that I was the vampire and you were human, and I wanted to make you a vampire too, but you didn't want to be a vampire."

"Your dream sounds rather bizarre, Edwin. Sometimes you can be quite peculiar."

"The dream started in a meadow with a small pond and a beautiful waterfall. By the time you woke me up I had this silly story about a vampire and a human teenager all worked out in my head. It's like a novel wrote itself in my dream."

"That sounds made up, Edwin."

"I know it seems ridiculous, but it's true, Jezebella."

"I'm sorry, Edwin, but that just sounds fake," Jezebella said as she gathered her books and headed for the door.

"I *swear*, Jezebella, that's exactly how it happened," I said, hurrying after her.

"If you say so, Edwin."

"Did I miss anything important in class?"

"Nothing important at all," Jezebella replied as we reached the door and joined the crowd of students in the hall.

"By the way, what time shall I pick you up for prom tomorrow?" I asked.

"At twilight," Jezebella replied.

Made in the USA
San Bernardino, CA
04 December 2015